THREE SILENT THINGS

THREE SILENT THINGS

Margaret Mayhew

severn House

British Library Cataloguing in Publication Data

Mayhew, Margaret, 1936-
  Three silent things
  1. Murder - Investigation - Fiction 2. Detective and
  mystery stories
  I. Title
  823.9'14[F]

ISBN-13: 978-0-7278-6677-6   (cased)

Except where actual historical events and characters are being
described for the storyline of this novel, all situations in this
publication are fictitious and any resemblance to living persons
is purely coincidental.

All Severn House titles are printed on acid-free paper.

Printed and bound in Great Britain by
MPG Books Ltd., Bodmin, Cornwall.

For Ella and Tilly

These be
Three silent things:
The falling snow . . . the hour
Before the dawn . . . the mouth of one
Just dead.

Adelaide Crapsey 1878–1914

One

It started to snow on New Year's Eve. The colonel stood at the sitting-room window of Pond Cottage as darkness was falling and watched the flakes float by and touch down without a sound. *These be three silent things: the falling snow . . . the hour before the dawn . . .* The first was very true, and so was the second – as he knew from sleepless nights, waiting for daybreak to come – but what was the third? He couldn't remember, nor where the words were from. They had come into his mind from out of the past – probably learned long ago at school.

The flakes settled thickly over the village green, snow on snow, snow on snow, and before long the green had turned to white. As it grew darker he drew the curtains and put another log on the fire. Thursday, the battle-scarred old cat that he had inherited along with the cottage and who had condescended to share his home, stretched and yawned and resettled himself comfortably in his place at the end of the sofa nearest the inglenook.

The colonel sat down in the tapestry wing-back chair on the other side of the fireplace and thought about the year ahead. He had faced the last eleven years alone since Laura had died and it seemed likely that he would face all the rest that remained to him in the same way, and at sixty-six there were probably still quite a number to go. It was something that he preferred not to think about too much, but New Year's Eve was a time for taking stock of one's life, and for looking back, as well as forward.

He had been living in Pond Cottage for nearly a year. Time had passed somehow and he had learned to deal with the solitude and the silence. They were spectres that he had succeeded in taming, if not in banishing. He counted his blessings: a married son and a daughter-in-law, a grandson and another grandchild on the way; a dear and loving daughter, successful and happy in her career. This nice old cottage in Frog End, a beautiful Dorset village; pleasant acquaintances he had made here; enough money not to have to worry too much about it; his health; his strength; his wits and his garden – which had turned out, in its making, to be an unexpected ally. Most people would say he was a very fortunate man in every respect except one – the one that mattered to him the most. He could no longer count Laura among his blessings – only the memory of her. Thank God, at least nobody could take that away.

Thinking of his children reminded him that he ought to ring them to wish them a Happy New Year. He dialled Marcus and Susan's number in Norfolk first and his daughter-in-law answered the phone.

'Happy New Year, Susan.'

'Oh, thank you, Father. And to you.'

He wished he could persuade her to call him Hugh; he had suggested it several times, but it seemed unlikely that she ever would. 'How are you all?'

'Well, Eric's running a temperature, so we're a bit worried about him. He's very touchy at the moment.'

When was he not? the colonel wondered, reflecting on his grandson's endless tantrums. 'How are *you*, Susan?'

'Well, I always feel awfully sick in the mornings . . . it was just the same expecting Eric, but the doctor thinks everything's all right.'

'That's good. Take care of yourself.'

It was the latest thing to say to people: take care. The new young postman who wore a baseball cap turned back to front and shorts in summer, kept telling him to do that, and so did others who could have no real interest in him doing so. He had an idea that it had come from across the Atlantic, rather on the lines of 'have a nice day'. In Susan's case, though, he *did* mean it. He couldn't help his lack of any real affection for her – that was beyond his control, as was his unfortunate aversion to his over-indulged and whingeing grandson – but he could wish her well, which he certainly did, and the child she was carrying. She was his son's wife and therefore a part of his own responsibility.

When Marcus had lost his job last year Susan had gone back to her mother and the marriage had been on the rocks. But now there was a new job and a new house and a new baby on the way. He had good reason to hope that the New Year would be a happy one for them.

He tried Alison's London number but got her answering machine and left a message in obedience to its crisp command. She had saved Christmas for him by coming down to the cottage, bearing gifts and a Fortnum's hamper and, most of all, bringing the gift of herself and her company. They had gone to church, eaten and drunk a great deal and played chess and cards by the fire. In the end, the dreaded event had passed almost painlessly. He had learned that Christmas could be a sad time, however much you tried to ignore it. The carols, the cards – even the tree that he and Alison had dutifully decorated – all conspired against you. There was no escape from bitter-sweet memories. Or from regrets.

He flicked through the January edition of the parish magazine. The new young vicar was exhorting his parishioners to give thought to their spiritual lives in the New Year, as well as to more temporal considerations such as new diets and summer holiday plans. There was to be a meeting of the Over-Sixties Club in the village hall on the tenth of January for a cup of tea and a sing-song; a jumble sale would be held in the hall later in the month, admission 50p, all contributions welcome; and there was to be a charity Quiz Night in the Dog and Duck, tickets £5 a head. Somebody was going to give a lecture, with slides, on The Dorset of Old and someone else had started up a Venture for Retired People aimed at '*discovering hidden talents and combating boredom and loneliness by getting involved in new activities, hobbies and studies. An exciting journey of self-discovery.*' A worthy notion if ever there was one, he thought, but somehow more depressing than uplifting.

As far as he knew, he had no hidden talents; the few he did have had already been discovered and put to use long ago. He had no particular hobbies either – unless listening to music and the radio or reading counted, and he didn't think they did. Nor did chess or card games. Occasionally the Cuthbertsons asked him over for a bridge evening which they took rather too seriously for his liking. The major, fortified by a large, and frequently replenished, glass of whisky at his elbow, fancied himself as the Omar Sharif of Frog End, but, in fact, Mrs Cuthbertson was a far better player.

No, hobbies meant actually *doing* things: making models, woodwork, throwing pots, collecting, painting . . . He'd taken up gardening, more or less because he'd had to unless he wanted to live surrounded by a jungle, but gardening was somehow in an altogether different category, as his green-fingered neighbour Naomi Grimshaw would certainly agree. So far as *she* was concerned, gardening was a way of life. Almost a religion. After all, a garden was considered an earthly paradise – in the right hands, of course. *'Tis very sure God walks in mine.* He had read those lines some-where. It was doubtful that God would care much for his, as yet, but he might well fancy a quiet stroll in Naomi's.

Maybe, he should go to cookery classes and learn to cook better. Naomi persisted in bombarding him with her misspelled recipes, and had ruthlessly outlawed instant meals-for-one from his fridge, carrying out snap inspec-tions that reminded him of his old sergeant-major at Sandhurst, but the truth was that he had no real interest in cooking for himself. A chop, a steak, a piece of grilled fish, scrambled eggs . . . he could manage those and some vegetables without too much bother. Often he simply opened a tin, following the bad example of his predecessor, old Ben, who had left a mountain of empty and rusty cans in the cottage back garden.

Perhaps he should join the Venture for Retired People and take up tapestry – a hobby that was, apparently, very popular with old soldiers. He could sit by the fire, stitching away at something useful – a chair seat or a kneeler for the church. The trouble was that his experience with a needle was strictly limited to sewing on buttons in the army and botching it up. Or maybe he could learn a new language – Mandarin, for instance, to add to his fluent French and German and to the very basic Cantonese and Malay he had picked up serving in Hong Kong and Singapore. The problem would be how to put Mandarin to any use in Frog End, and his days of being sent off to the Far East to serve his country were over. How about painting? There was plenty to paint in Dorset – beautiful countryside, quaint old thatched cottages, ancient manors, fields, woods, streams, bridges, a wonderful coastline . . . the snag was that he'd never been any good at art and he doubted if there would be much pleasure or satisfaction in doing it badly.

He set aside the magazine and listened to one of his old Gilbert and Sullivan records to raise his spirits.

Behold the Lord High Executioner,
A personage of noble rank and title.
A dignified and potent officer
Whose functions are particularly vital.
Defer, defer to the Lord High Executioner . . .

The colonel beat in time with his fingers against the chair arm. Alison had wanted him to get compact discs and a new, state-of-the-art player with loudspeakers posted around the room, but, so far, he had resisted. He supposed that when the vinyl records eventually became impossibly scratched and ancient he would succumb. No good setting his face against change. One must move with the times.

At eleven o'clock he primed the whisky decanter, got out glasses, and filled a small jug with water in readiness for his neighbour. Soon after, he heard her pounding at the front door. Naomi Grimshaw stamped into the hallway, swathed in a voluminous red wool cape and shedding snow from her moon boot trainers. Her thatch of short grey hair was adorned with large white flakes which she shook off like a dog as she unfurled the cape in the swirling movement of a matador in the bull-ring, revealing a neon pink tracksuit beneath.

'Bloody awful night, Hugh. The damned stuff's already a foot deep. If it goes on at this rate, we'll be snowed in. Brought you a New Year offering, by the way.' She thrust a jam jar at him. 'Not one of my best efforts but it's edible.'

The jar bore a crooked label and he deciphered Naomi's scrawl: *Rubarb & Ginger.* He smiled; it would be a tragedy if she ever learned to spell.

'That's very kind – thank you. Come and sit down. The fire's going rather well.'

In the sitting room she rubbed her hands at the sight of both the blazing log fire and the whisky decanter. 'Ah . . . just what the doctor ordered.'

She picked up Thursday and deposited him firmly at the other end of the sofa, taking over his place close to the fire. If a cat's look could kill, the colonel thought, amused, Naomi would have fallen stone dead. He poured out her usual stiff measure with a splash of water – no ice, which she considered a waste of space – and handed her the glass. She encircled it with her large, rough gardener's hand and sniffed at it appreciatively.

'Good old Chivas! Wish I could afford it. Thank God you don't get any of that other rubbish, Hugh. It's a real pleasure having you for a neighbour. Down the hatch.'

He sat in his wing-back chair with his own drink – no ice, no water. A Scot would have approved. Thursday was re-settling himself huffily, still casting baleful glances in Naomi's direction.

'Did your son and his family get off all right?'

'Allah be praised, yes. Loved having them but I'd had enough. The cottage is too small and the kids are too noisy and my Aussie daughter-in-law never stops complaining about the English weather. As though it never, *ever* rains in Sydney. Lucky they left before it started snowing. They'll be on the way back to their summer now. Extraordinary to think of it. Talk about upside down.'

'When will you see them again?'

'Maybe not till next Christmas – *if* they come over again. Or I might go there, if I can face the flight. I'd sooner go over in the summer, though – *our* summer. It'd be cooler there then. Can't stand the heat.' She studied him over the rim of her glass. 'You're looking well, Hugh. *Much better than when you first came here* – you were miserable then. I was quite worried. Frog End must suit you. I was afraid you'd find it too dull after your rolling-stone army life.'

He smiled drily. 'I wouldn't call it dull exactly. Not every village can boast a real-live murder – if that isn't a contradiction in terms.'[1]

'Huh. That's true. Poor old Ursula got what she deserved, though. She was a bitch. Not a single wet eye at her funeral. Everyone was delighted to see the back of her – except for Ruth, of course. She's the one I felt very sorry for. It can't have been much fun having Ursula for a mother and then having her bumped-off like that.'

'She's planning to stay on at the Manor, I gather.'

'Looks like it. Rattling around in the place, but that state of affairs may change eventually. Our nice young doctor is very attentive there, have you noticed? Ruth's not playing ball, though – there's a rumour of some old love affair she still hasn't got over – but Tom Harvey's the persistent type. He'll bide his time if he's any sense, and I'm quite sure he has. She's going to open a sort of garden centre there – did you hear that morsel on the grapevine? Selling plants she's raised. Not like those frightful places that don't grow any of their own stuff and cart it all over from the Continent. She's asked me if I'll help a bit getting it off the ground – pass on a few tips. Give the odd talk . . . you know the sort of thing. How To Prune Your Roses, Planning Your Herbaceous Border, Choosing The Right Shrub . . . nothing too airy-fairy. Down to earth stuff.'

He got up to put another log on the fire. It flared up, crackled and then settled. He prodded around with the poker, making more flames.

'She couldn't ask for anyone better qualified.'

'Thank you for those kind words. Speaking of gardens, Hugh, how's yours?'

_____

1. See *Old Soldiers Never Die*

'Well . . . covered with snow at the moment, like they all are. I have to admit I haven't done a thing lately. Not for several weeks, in fact. I'm afraid I never even finished sweeping up the leaves.'

'Oh, leave the bloody leaves – I never bother much with 'em. They'll rot down nicely and they give shelter to some useful creepy crawlies – little chaps you'll want there on your side after the winter. Snails too, unfortunately, but you can always deal with those later on.'

He sat down again. 'Poison them, you mean?'

'God, no! I never use anything like that. Don't agree with it. I simply move the damn things out of the garden. Put them all in a bucket and dump them somewhere else. People say they always come back but if they do, I just take 'em out again. No, now's the time to do a spot of planning ahead. Spring'll be here before you know it and you want to be thinking about what improvements you're going to make. The winter's best for doing that because you can see the skeleton of the garden, as it were – the bare bones of it. See where it could do with some more flesh, or whether things need changing around or getting rid of. Out with anything that doesn't pay its way – that's my motto. Be ruthless. Soon as the snow's gone, take a jolly good look. How about planting some marsh marigolds in that damp corner by your pond?'

'If you think it's a good idea.'

What little he knew about gardening, he had mostly learned from his neighbour. When he had bought the cottage he had known less than nothing and cared not a jot, but little by little she had inspired him with her unbounded enthusiasm and her knowledge and, with her help, he had gradually turned his own long-neglected tangle of nettles and brambles and old tin cans into the beginnings of an attractive garden. The lost pond had been rediscovered and dredged, some plants carefully rescued, others ruthlessly uprooted, new ones put in, according to the advice offered. Her own garden was, to his mind, a model of what a country cottage garden should be – apparently semi-wild. Not a straight line or any geometrically sharp edges in sight. Plants seemed simply to grow where they had seeded – in beds, along paths, between stones, cascading down old stone walls, climbing up others. He had discovered, though, that, in reality, Naomi kept a tight grip on nature and knew exactly what she was about.

'Well, they're nice things and they'll love the mud. Or *Darmera peltata*. That's another good marsh plant and it doesn't spread too quickly. Rather pretty pink flowers. And you might consider putting some water lilies in the pond – give those frogs of yours somewhere to sit.'

The single frog who had made his home in the recovered pond last summer had become several frogs – much to his pleasure and satisfaction. After all, the village was called Frog End.

'The other half, Naomi?'

She tipped up her glass. 'Don't mind if I do.'

He poured her another hefty shot and added a splash of water. 'They seem to have done a fairly decent job of converting your former home. I hear all the flats have been taken.'

She grunted. 'I can't bear to see the poor old place myself – always look the other way whenever I'm driving past. It's a bit of a Victorian horror, of course, but we loved it. If my sister and I had known we were selling to some property developer we'd never have let it go. We thought he was going to live in it – fools that we were. He never said a word about turning it into flats. Paid us a pittance, too, the twister.'

'I'm afraid it's the fate of a lot of big houses these days. Even if you *had* sold it as a private home, the next buyer would probably have turned it into flats just the same. Or knocked it down and built a dozen prestigious executive houses on the land.'

'Is that supposed to comfort me? But I expect you're right, Hugh. Anyway, we couldn't stay. Needed an army of servants and gardeners to run it and a fortune to keep it in order and stop it falling down. God knows what it would have cost to heat it properly. We never did in our day. Jessica and I lived in the kitchen with the Aga when we were there on our own – before she died.'

He topped up his own drink. 'I'm due to rattle a collecting tin round there tomorrow, so I'll let you know what it's like inside.'

'Who's roped you in to do that?'

'Miss Butler. Major Cuthbertson usually does that end of the village but he's down with flu apparently.'

'Down with a hangover more like. I damn nearly collided with him coming back from Dorchester the other day. He's an absolute menace now he's got his driving licence back.'

The colonel suppressed a smile at the pot calling the kettle black. Personally, he would sooner not encounter either of them on the roads – Naomi crouched fiercely behind the wheel of her fire-engine red Metro or the major finally restored to the controls of his Escort after a year-long ban.

'I'm rather wondering how successful I'll be collecting. It's in aid of donkeys. A Save the Donkey campaign. Miss Butler says that there are a great many that need saving in this country, not just abroad.'

'I'll bet there are! People buy them for their spoiled kids and then get tired of them. Forget they need feeding and looking after and company. I'll put something in your tin, Hugh, but I wouldn't count on the people in those flats at the Hall. Never see a sign of them round the village. All London types, I should think. Probably never set eyes on a donkey except on one of those awful foreign holidays they all go on.' Naomi switched subjects abruptly. 'Tell me, what do you think of our new vicar?'

He said cautiously, 'He seems nice enough.'

Naomi snorted. 'Can't stand the type myself. Beard and sandals, guitars in church, happy-clappy, shaking hands with your neighbour and all that nonsense. He'll try and get us using that New Series next. Over my dead body – and everybody's else's, I should think. I can't see Ruth allowing it. She'd know how we'd all feel.'

'Does she have any say in the matter?'

'Well, the living's in her name now. Surely she could veto it?'

'I rather think the nearest bishop might be the one who decides those sort of things.'

'God help us if you're right, Hugh. They're as bad as the rest, these days. They pander to all these guitar people because they want to be seen as trendy. All they do is scare off the faithful oldies who still go to church, and they're not many of those left.'

He glanced at the grandfather clock in the corner of the sitting room and saw that its hands were close to midnight.

'Nearly time.'

He got up to open the lattice window. It was still snowing and the outside air was ice cold, the silence complete – so complete that he felt that he could have reached out and touched it. *These be three silent things . . . the falling snow, the hour before dawn . . .* he still couldn't think of the third one. Behind him the grandfather clock began its twelve silvery chimes and, as they stopped, the village church bells broke the silence outside, ringing out loudly across the snow. He turned to raise his glass.

'Happy New Year, Naomi.'

'Happy New Year, Hugh. Hope it's a specially good one for us both. Though they're all pretty much the same these days.'

Two

It must have snowed for most of the night because when the colonel drew back his bedroom curtains in the morning, a thick white blanket of the stuff was shrouding the garden and frosting the bare branches. The sun's first rays emerging over the wood behind the cottage made the scene glitter like a cheap Christmas card.

Thursday had to be prised from his place on the sofa, claws forcibly detached one by one from the cushion, before he could be put outside the back door. There was a perfectly good cat flap that the colonel had had installed but the old cat couldn't be bothered to use it if there was someone around to open and shut the door for him. He stood there in the deep snow, torn ears flattened, a front paw lifted in horror and disgust.

The colonel shaved, bathed and dressed before he boiled himself an egg – timed for four and a half minutes – and made himself toast and coffee. The disciplined army years had made the idea of slopping around in a dressing-gown unthinkable. When he had eaten the egg and the toast he stood at the window for a while, drinking his coffee and looking out at the garden.

Some animal had left neat tracks in the virgin snow across the lawn – a fox probably rather than a badger, and certainly not Thursday who was still crouched resentfully close to the door. Somewhere under the pristine white blanket the plants were sleeping their long winter sleep, including all those bulbs – daffodils and the narcissi – that he had installed so laboriously in the long grass by the apple trees last autumn. He had ordered them from a catalogue and when they had arrived he'd taken yet another leaf out of Naomi's gardening book and chucked them down anyhow, and wherever they had fallen he had buried them. No regimented ranks allowed. At the back of the same catalogue he had come across illustrations of snowdrops – he'd had no idea that so many types existed – and another evening had passed pleasantly beside the fire while he made his choices. The common snowdrop, *Galanthus nivalis,* and some charming variations: *Galanthus Merlin* with its green inner; the yellow-centred *Wendy's Gold*; *Magnet* with a single flower on a long stem, said to shimmer in the breeze; *Ophelia*, a double flower with outer petals lifted like wings; *Augustus*, which had wrinkled petals and pleated leaves. He had planted them in a sort of fairy ring around the white lilac where they would now be waiting off-stage, metaphorically speaking, to make their brave entrance – the first act in a long and ever-changing variety show that would play until the return of winter.

He washed up the breakfast things and put them to dry in the rack.

The army had trained him for many things, but not for domesticity, and after Laura had died he had learned the hard way. Beds he could make with military precision, shirts he could iron without a crease, brass and silver he could polish brightly, shoes he could shine to look like glass; but he had had to learn to clean and scour and dust and vacuum, and how to work a washing machine. With Naomi's brisk encouragement and charmingly misspelled recipes, he had taught himself to cook simple dishes and tried to avoid the tins or microwaving meals-for-one, though he did not always succeed.

Miss Butler had delivered the collection tin the day before, together with the cardboard tray of *Save the Donkey* badges and a box of pins. A paper wrapper round the tin showed a photograph of a very sad-looking donkey with drooping ears, matted coat and sticking-out bones, and loaded with a horrifyingly heavy burden. The badges carried the picture of the same donkey's head.

Freda Butler had clearly taken the cause very much to her heart.

'Poor creatures. So cruelly treated – even here, in our own dear England, Colonel, where people ought to know better. We don't use them as beasts of burden, of course, or work them to death, but there are some quite shocking cases of neglect and mistreatment, you know. You wouldn't believe it.'

'Oh, I think I would,' he had said, having come across a great deal of mindless cruelty in his life. 'Tell me, how exactly does the fund manage to save them?' He felt he ought to know, in case somebody asked.

'Well, it pays for mobile veterinary clinics overseas to help the poor suffering animals there. They find donkeys just left to die on the side of the road, you know, once they're too weak to work any more. Quite shocking! And there are some lovely sanctuaries in this country where the ones that have been badly treated or abandoned can live out their days in peace and comfort. They are always in need of funds.'

'It all sounds very worthwhile.'

'Yes, indeed. The trouble is people don't seem to care about donkeys very much. Horses and dogs, yes, and cats, too, of course, but not poor old donkeys. Considering that Our Lord rode into Jerusalem on one, you'd think they might give them more consideration and respect, wouldn't you?'

He had agreed with her, though it was a long time since he had believed in the Lord. Not since he had watched Laura die slowly in pain and misery. But Miss Butler patently did. She was one of the legions of decent, faithful people who still went to church every Sunday, who dutifully echoed the beautiful words, chanted the Creed and sang the glorious hymns. One of the faithful oldies referred to by Naomi.

'Well, I hope I won't let you or the donkeys down.'

She had sighed. 'I'm afraid you'll find some people reluctant to donate much – just a few pence. They slip it into the tin very quickly so you can't see how little it is but I can always tell by the sound it makes. Sometimes they won't even answer the door at all. Of course, they might take more notice of you, Colonel. I don't think Major Cuthbertson ever tried very hard. He always went round very quickly.'

'I'll do my best,' he had promised her.

'I know you will, Colonel. I can see that you have great compassion for God's less fortunate creatures.'

They had both looked at the inert lump of black and tan fur on the sofa.

He had said, 'Thursday seems to have taken me on permanently.'

'It's an unusual name.'

'I gather he originally turned up on a Thursday when old Ben was living here and so he called him that. He disappeared after Ben died and then reappeared when I moved in – on another Thursday, by coincidence.'

'Yes, I saw him. Cats are strange creatures. They always know what's best for them.'

'They're survivors, Miss Butler,' he had said with a smile. 'And rather better at it than donkeys.'

He had watched the elderly spinster pick her way down the snowy path and out of the gate. A timid soul dressed invariably in navy blue – a nod perhaps to her long service in the Wrens – who lived in a cottage even smaller than his own on the opposite side of the village green. Her sitting-room window provided her with an unrivalled view of all the village comings and goings – which would have been how she had spotted Thursday's reappearance when he had moved into the cottage. He had sometimes caught the glint of the powerful Zeiss binoculars, rumoured to have formerly belonged to a German U-boat commander and appropriated by her late father, an admiral, and which it was known that she used to see farther and better. Not that she was a malicious gossip. Far from it. She merely observed; and, doubtless, deduced.

He opened the back door to let Thursday in. The cat stalked past, flicking clumps of snow fastidiously from his paws, and sat down in front of his empty bowl. Breakfast was served. Fresh chicken mixed with a little liver, chopped small enough for the few remaining teeth and moistened with warm water from the kettle. Thursday sniffed at it critically before deigning to begin. It was a mystery how the old cat, who had almost certainly lived rough in his pre-Pond Cottage days, had acquired such pampered and picky tastes.

The colonel put on his heavy tweed overcoat, cap, scarf, gloves and boots and hung the Save the Donkey tray by its webbing strap around his neck. The collection tin already contained Naomi's contribution and he added more coins of his own so that it made an encouraging rattle.

Outside, it was crisp and very cold; the snow sparkled in the sunlight and squeaked beneath his boots and his breath clouded the air. The cold didn't worry him; he'd known far worse during his time serving in Berlin and, on the whole, he preferred it to the energy-sapping effects of tropical heat. He set off briskly on the route that Miss Butler had allotted him – the Dog and Duck; the beautiful old stone cottages clustered round the green; the cul-de-sac of new bungalows; the Vicarage; the Manor and finishing up at the Hall – Naomi's former childhood home, bought for a song by the canny developer and turned into flats.

He started off at the Dog and Duck – probably the reverse order of the Major's route. The pub was still shut but the landlord's wife, Sheila, was busy with the vacuum cleaner in the public bar, pushing it to and fro across the red and green patterned carpet that had been laid over the old flag-stones. The Dog and Duck, once a simple place of real ale, ham and cheese sandwiches and packets of Smith's crisps, had moved with the times. The beer now came out of pipes and bottles and full meals were served in the dining-room extension. There was a good deal of very shiny new copper and brass and wipe-clean plastic. The Christmas decorations were still up – swags of fake holly nailed along the beams, the Christmas tree beside the inglenook decorated with pretend presents, silver and gold tinsel and winking coloured lights.

He rattled his collection tin and Sheila turned off the vacuum cleaner.

'What's it for, Colonel?'

'Donkeys,' he said. 'A lot of them need saving.'

'Well, that makes a change. It's usually for people in countries you've never heard of and you wonder if they ever get a penny.' She came over and picked up a badge. 'Poor old thing, he looks really miserable. Like nobody's said a kind word to him in his life. I'll get my purse.'

She put several coins in the tin and he thanked her.

'Sorry I interrupted you.'

She smiled at him in her friendly way – a thoroughly decent woman who worked like a dog, helping her husband to run the pub. He marvelled at how they stood the long hours, the physical grind, the effort of being nice to every customer every time.

'Don't worry about that, Colonel. I doubt if we'll be busy today. Not with the snow. And they say there's more to come.'

He trudged on towards the first of the old cottages on his route where old Mrs Peabody, who had to be at least ninety-nine, beckoned him into her sitting room. He stood, trying not to let the snow fall from his boots on to the threadbare carpet, while she searched in vain for her purse.

'I put it somewhere, I know I did . . . let's see now, it might be behind a cushion . . . or sometimes I put it away in a drawer.'

In the end he found it for her on the mantelpiece behind the clock and she insisted on him taking out a pound coin.

'That's rather a lot, Mrs Peabody.'

'Nonsense. I don't need much – not at my time of life. Besides, you know the old saying.'

'Which one?'

She wagged a gnarled finger at him. 'It's in giving that we receive.'

What a dear old soul, he thought, as he made his way on to the next cottage where some children were shrieking and laughing as they built a snowman in the front garden – a carrot for the nose, stones for eyes, a bent stick for the mouth. He was rather a fine-looking snowman – very portly, as snowmen should be. As the colonel admired him, the children's mother came out with an old hat to complete the outfit and there were more shrieks and laughter.

He knocked on the next front door, but without much hope. The owners lived in London and only came down for occasional weekends during the summer. They were probably sunning themselves on some Caribbean beach, or skiing in Austria. Two of the other cottages were also second homes and rarely used. High prices had been paid and a good deal of money spent on modernization. Out with the old stone sink, the ancient range, the claw-foot bath and the poky Victorian grate; away with the privy shed and the tumble-down hen house. In with the modern plumbing and wiring, the central heating, the gleaming bathroom and the country kitchen copied faithfully from a magazine – accurate down to the Aga, the scrubbed-pine table and the wicker basket artfully filled with corn stalks and dried flowers. He had done much the same himself with Pond Cottage – except for the country kitchen – but at least he lived in the place.

By the time he reached the end of the cottages the tin was making quite a satisfactory rattle. So far, Miss Butler seemed to have been mistaken about the donkeys' appeal.

'I hear the colonel's taken over your collection round, Roger,' Marjorie Cuthbertson said.

'Has he?'

'Freda Butler told me. Let's hope he makes a better job of it than you usually do. That shouldn't be too difficult for him.'

Major Cuthbertson, seated by the electric fire in the living room of Shangri-La with *The Times* newspaper held up like a shield in front of his face, gave a grunt. 'Not my fault. Couldn't possibly have done it with this damn flu I've picked up.'

'You don't seem very ill to me.'

'Well, I jolly well feel it,' he said in injured tones, turning a page of the newspaper. 'Asking for trouble to go out in this sort of weather. I'd have got pneumonia, or something. Not that you'd mind.'

'Don't be absurd, Roger. Of course, I'd mind. You'd be a perfect nuisance if you were really ill.'

His wife had the constitution of an ox, he thought bitterly.

In all the years that they had been married – and it seemed like a hell of a lot of them – he could only remember her being under the weather a couple of times, whereas he was always going down with some damned bug or other, not to mention the old malaria that he'd picked up in the Far East and which kept coming back like a song. Of course, Marjorie didn't believe in any of it; so far as she was concerned he was either malingering or he'd drunk too much. Sometimes, he thought wistfully of how nice it would be to have a wife who nursed him tenderly when he was ill, who stroked his fevered brow and spoke to him in a soft and sympathetic voice. He raised *The Times* a few inches. It was no damn good now they'd made it the size of one of those tabloids: Marjorie could see him over the top easily. And, anyway, most of it was rubbish these days: scandal, gossip, celebrities . . . not a decent article in it. He might as well take the *Sun*. To think it had once been a newspaper to be proud of, the envy of the world – like the BBC.

He said, 'I might have given it to other people.'

'Given what?'

'My flu.'

She gave a laugh that sounded like a guard dog's bark. 'Well, you'll be sorry you didn't do this one.'

'It's only for donkeys.'

'I'm not talking about *them*. Guess who's living at the Hall now?'

'No idea.'

'One of your old pin-ups. Lois Delaney.'

The Times collapsed, crackling on to his lap. 'Did you say Lois Delaney?'

'Are you going deaf, Roger? Yes, I said Lois Delaney. She's moved into one of the flats.'

He stared, goggle-eyed. 'How do you know?'

'Leslie told me when I went to have my hair done last time. He'd just heard it from somebody.'

Once a week his wife aimed the Escort at Dorchester to have her hair washed and set in the style that she had worn since the major had first met her.

'But why on *earth* would she want to live at Frog End?'

Marjorie Cuthbertson shrugged. 'Perhaps she wants to be left alone, like that Garbo woman. She's in the middle of getting divorced, apparently.' She smiled grimly. 'Anyway, you've missed your chance, Roger. Just think, you could have met her if it hadn't been for your flu.'

With that parting shot, his wife left the room and the major was left alone with his thoughts, and his regrets. *Lois Delaney!* He'd been a fan ever since he could remember. Seen her on the stage dozens of times. In his youth – pre-Marjorie – he'd been a bit of a stage door Johnnie and gone round to wait for her to come out afterwards. Once, he'd given her a bunch of red roses and she'd given him a wonderful smile in return. Spoken to him, too. Just a few words and he could never remember what she'd actually said, but it had been something jolly nice. He'd never seen such a beautiful woman before, or since. Of course, she'd be getting on a bit now, but he'd take a bet that she was still a corker. Better not let Marjorie get any inkling about that little episode of the roses. Look at the way she'd cottoned on to him and Ursula Swynford. She'd made a joke of it, of course – roared with laughter, in fact – but he could tell she'd been pretty jealous. Not there'd been anything to be jealous of – someone had gone and bumped-off Ursula before it could happen.

Of course, Lois Delaney was in another class altogether. His heart picked up speed. To think that he might have met her again if he'd gone out collecting for those damned donkeys! He could picture the scene. She'd have opened her flat door and he'd have bowed and smiled in a smooth, man-of-the-world way so she'd have known at once that he wasn't just some country bumpkin. They'd have got talking and she'd have been flattered and impressed to hear that he had seen her act so many times. He'd have reminded her about the bunch of red roses, which she was sure to remember. And hadn't Marjorie said she was getting divorced? Who knows, one thing might have led to another . . .

Major Cuthbertson clutched at his throat. He needed a drink badly. Something to steady him. Medicinal, of course.

It wouldn't do to get all het-up in his weakened condition. The ticker needed watching at his age – though, of course, there was plenty of life left in the old dog yet. After all, an old fiddle was more in tune, autumn was just as nice as spring, and an old flame still had lots of sparks.

Marjorie had gone off to the kitchen and would be banging pots around doing what she always called 'something about lunch'. He hoped to God it wouldn't be yesterday's supper reheated: it had been bad enough the first time round. They'd always had someone to cook for them abroad and when they finally came home to Blighty the old girl had never seemed to get the hang of it. She'd be out of the room for quite a while so, if he was quick and quiet, he could have a stiffener.

He laid down *The Times* quietly and tiptoed across the living room to the musical cocktail cabinet which he had been given on his retirement from the regiment. The damned thing played the same bloody tune every time it was opened. He had never found out how to disconnect it but he'd learned to get the whisky out faster than Wyatt Earp drawing his gun. He lifted the lid, grabbed the bottle by the neck and shut the lid again, cutting *Drink to me only with thine eyes* off short. A decent slug in the glass and the bottle was back again with only a few more notes played. Major Cuthbertson sat down again, took a gulp and leaned back with his eyes closed. Lois Delaney all those years ago . . . the red roses, that wonderful smile she had given him when he'd been a dapper young blade, foot-loose and fancy free. He sighed. By Jove, those were the days!

The colonel walked on towards the bungalows beyond the green. When he had been looking for somewhere to live in Frog End he had almost bought one of them – aptly named Journey's End. They all had rust-free plastic guttering and plastic down-pipes, rot-proof metal-framed windows and very small, easy-maintenance gardens. Instead, he had chosen the near-derelict Pond Cottage with all its expensive shortcomings and its acre of impenetrable jungle.

As he entered the horseshoe-shaped cul-de-sac, Dr Harvey,
the local GP was driving out. He lowered his car window.
'Don't go and break a leg, Colonel. It's very slippery.'
'I hear there's more to come.'
'Heaven help us . . . this is bad enough.'
Tom Harvey waved and drove on, his car crunching slowly
through the snow. Naomi's nice young doctor who had
helped him through the black dog days when he had first
come to live at Frog End, warning him off the addictive
sleeping pills and pointing out that he still had a useful life
ahead of him. And he had discovered that he did have his
uses when he had helped to clear up the mystery of Lady
Swynford's murder at the Manor fête. He hoped that her
daughter, Ruth, would eventually come to her senses and
realize what a worthy suitor she had.

The bungalows were mainly occupied by people who
were, indeed, coming to the end of their journey through
life: retired couples who had chosen to move to the country,
to live on one convenient level and cultivate a very small
and very flat garden. The houses were more or less identical
– same shape; same windows; same size gardens, front and
back; small up-and-over garage to one side; sunburst iron
gates and a concrete pathway leading up to the front
door, flanked by narrow flower beds. The only differences
were in the individual paint colours and in the gardens
themselves. Some, he had observed, walking by on other
occasions, were weed-free models of order; others were
brave attempts, and one or two were downright neglected.
At the moment, of course, they were all covered uniformly
with a heavy layer of snow, except for the red top of a
gnome's hat poking up through the white. No children, no
shrieks of merriment, no fat snowman taking form.

He made his way round anticlockwise, starting with the
one ironically called Tree Tops. A pleasant, elderly woman
answered the door and fetched her handbag. He wondered
whether the bungalow's name had been her personal choice?
A childhood spent in Kenya, perhaps? Or Rhodesia? Or
South Africa? A wooden house built high in the trees beside
a water-hole or overlooking the grassy veldt?

Net curtains twitched as he opened more sunburst gates and he knew that he was being watched. Out of the next five bungalows only two answered the ding-dong chimes at the door, though he was fairly certain that everybody was at home. One old man who opened his door declined to do the same with his wallet.

'Donkeys? That's the RSPCA's job, isn't it? And they've got enough money already. What about ex-servicemen? Nobody cares about us. The army pension's a disgrace.'

'I quite agree,' he said amicably. 'I'm an army man myself. But that's rather up to the Government, isn't it?' He gave the tin a good rattle. 'Some donkeys don't have much of a life. And every little helps.'

Reluctantly, a few coins were fished out of a trouser pocket and slid into the tin in the furtive way that Miss Butler had described.

The colonel raised his cap. 'Thank you, sir. Very generous of you.'

The next three – all women – were quite sorry for the donkey and the tin grew heavier. The last of the ten bunga-lows was Shangri-La – residence of Major and Mrs Cuthbertson. He hesitated for a moment before ringing the bell, bearing in mind that the Major was ill, but it was unlikely that even Mrs Cuthbertson would have attempted to drive in the snow and so she would be there to answer the door. It was opened, in fact, by the major himself – not lying on his sick-bed but fully dressed.

'Good to see you, old chap. Come on in.'

'I don't think I'd better – not with these boots. Your wife might not be too pleased.'

'Nonsense . . . Marjorie won't mind. Anyway, she's busy with lunch.'

He stepped over the threshold and into the narrow hallway. Shangri-La was an even less appropriate name than Tree Tops. There was no suggestion whatever of the mystical or exotic about its sombrely furnished interior; no hint of an idyllic and hidden paradise discovered at last, no fragrance of blossom or sandalwood. Only a smell of something burning wafting from the kitchen.

He rattled the tin gently. 'I just wondered if you'd like to make a contribution.'

'Of course. Glad to help the donkeys. Damned good cause, if you ask me.' The major foraged in his pocket and dropped several noisy coins into the tin. 'How's it going?'

'Pretty well. I've still got the Vicarage and the Manor to do, then I finish up at the Hall.'

'As a matter of fact, old chap, I was going to ask if you'd like me to take over? I'm feeling a lot better this morning. I'd be glad to.'

The colonel shook his head. 'There's no need. I'm rather enjoying it, to tell you the truth. And it wouldn't do your flu much good.'

'Nonsense. Could do with a bit of fresh air. Stretch the old legs. Change of scene, and all that. So, if you'd like to hand over the stuff I'll see to the rest.'

The colonel said firmly, 'I really don't think that's a good idea. And I don't think your wife would either.' He moved the collecting tin up out of the major's grasp and opened the front door behind him. 'I'd stay in the warm, if I were you.'

As he went down the path he wondered why on earth the major had suddenly been so anxious to do his bit. A guilty conscience, maybe? He obviously wasn't very ill. Or perhaps he just wanted a break from Mrs Cuthbertson – you couldn't blame him for that – and the chance to nip into the Dog and Duck? That was the trouble with faking sickness, there was usually a penalty to pay. He'd never tried it himself, but he'd come across men in the army who'd made a career out of malingering. As he reached the gate, he realized that he had forgotten to give out a donkey badge. It was too late, though, the door to Shangri-La had shut.

The major sat down again by the fire. Dammit, he'd made a complete hash of it. He should have been more forceful. Grabbed the tin out of his hand and the tray off his neck – except that the colonel was a tall chap, so it wouldn't have been easy. And he hadn't reckoned on him being so keen. Odd, that! He couldn't stand the collecting job himself – everyone hiding behind the curtains or slipping in two pence. Every time Miss Butler asked him to do it for some damn thing or other he tried to think of some excuse, but she had a way of getting round him. *Just this once, Major. It would be so kind of you and it's for a very good cause.* It was *always* a good cause, according to her, but he'd drawn the line at collecting for bloody donkeys. A fellow had his limits, after all, and that had been one of his.

Hang on a tick! The unwelcome thought had suddenly entered his mind that the colonel might have heard about Lois Delaney living at the Hall – which would explain why he was so hell-bent on going there himself. There was no denying that he was a younger man – not by much, of course – and taller, too, and he'd kept all his hair which was always an advantage. He outranked him, as well, unfortunately. The ladies always seemed to like the fellow, he'd noticed. Furthermore, he was a widower, so there was no wife in the background to put a spanner in the works, so to speak. The major ground his teeth. No question about it, the colonel could get a head start on him and there was no way he could think of to head him off at the pass.

Marjorie came stumping into the room, rattling the ornaments.

'Who was that at the door?'

'Just the colonel, doing the collection. I gave him something, of course.'

'A decent amount, I hope.'

'Naturally. I offered to take over the rest of the round for him. He wouldn't hear of it, though.'

'I expect he was worried about your flu.'

He ignored the sarcasm. 'He did mention that. I would have done it, though.'

'Of course you would, now you know that Lois Delaney is living at the Hall. Honestly, Roger, you don't imagine that she'd be interested in *you*, do you?'

He said stiffly. 'I did meet her once, you know. Years ago. She was very charming to me.'

Another of her barking laughs. 'She'd be charming to all

her fans. But don't fool yourself – she wouldn't remember you from Adam.'

While his wife went off to do something else about the lunch, the major took the opportunity to revisit the cock-tail bar for another quick pick-me-up. He needed to stiffen the old sinews and summon up the blood if he was going to manage to outpace the colonel.

The Vicarage door was opened by the new vicar's wife. She looked very young and very tired and very flustered, with a small baby in her arms and a toddler clinging to her leg. The vicar was out, apparently, calling on a sick parishioner. The colonel showed her the donkey tin and she disappeared for a long time before returning with a small handful of coins, several of which she then dropped on the doorstep. As he bent to help retrieve them, the baby started to cry, the toddler to yell and the telephone to ring insistently in the hall behind her.

'I'm very sorry it isn't more,' she shouted above the racket. 'I couldn't find very much.'

'Every little helps. Thank you.'

He raised his cap to her as he left, thinking that she was much too young and inexperienced to cope with the demands of the job. Vicars' wives needed to be tough to survive.

His next call was at the village Manor, a beautiful mullion-windowed, Jacobean house surrounded by a high stone wall. Walking up the long drive, he remembered the first time he had seen the place. He had taken on the job of Treasurer to the Summer Fête Committee which convened at the Manor – a job he had suspected quite rightly that nobody else wanted, but it had had the advantage of giving him something to do and, in doing it, of meeting village people. Meeting the Manor's then owner, the since-deceased Lady Swynford, had not, in truth, been much of a pleasure but her daughter, Ruth, was a different matter.

He reached the front door and tugged at the iron bell pull. It jangled somewhere in the depths of the house. He could hear a dog yapping – Lady Swynford's black French poodle, Shoo-Shoo. Ruth Swynford opened the door, the dog at her heels.

'How nice to see you, Colonel . . . do come in.'

He went into the hall, stamping his boots on the mat. The poodle jumped around him, wagging its tail. Lady Swynford had always had the wretched animal clipped into ridiculous pom-pom arrangements but Ruth had left its coat to grow naturally. It was certainly an improvement, though he doubted if he would ever feel warmly towards the creature.

'I won't come any further in, Ruth. I'm very snowy.'

She smiled up at him. 'The flagstones won't mind, and nor will I. I'm surprised to see you, Colonel. Major Cuthbertson usually does this beat. I suppose he thought up some excuse.'

'He's got flu.'

'Hmmm. Would you like some tea or coffee to warm you up?'

'Thank you, but no.'

'In that case, I'll fetch some money to buy one of your badges.'

She went away and came back with her purse; no coins, this time, but a folded note that she stuffed into the tin.

He handed over her badge. 'That's very generous of you, Ruth.'

She pinned the badge carefully on to her navy blue jumper. 'It's a very good cause. I've always liked donkeys. I used to keep a sweet old thing in the field when I was a child and he'd been rescued from some awful place. He died eventually and I cried buckets. Maybe I should get another one, now that I live down here.'

He looked at her with approval. Dressed in faded jeans and Fair Isle jumper, no make-up, freckles, a simple bob, she was very attractive in his eyes and, more to the point, a very nice person. Honest, intelligent, unpretentious, kind. The very opposite of her late mother. By her invitation, he now called her Ruth, but she still addressed him always as Colonel. No doubt she felt his ancient years required that formality.

He said, 'I heard a rumour that you might be selling some of your plants.'

'Who told you that?'

'My neighbour.'

She smiled. 'Trust Naomi to spill the beans. It *is* true but I'm not exactly up and running yet. I've had the idea simmering for ages but it still needs some working out. Do you think it's a good one?'

'I certainly do. If the plants you sell are anything like the ones in your garden, you'll have long queues.'

'Naomi's says she'll help me – give me advice and so on.'

'Then you can't lose with two sets of green fingers.'

She laughed and held out her broken-nailed hands. 'I don't know about green – more like black. Actually, I didn't care a damn about gardening before – not till I came back from London to look after my mother. Now it's an absolute passion.'

He wondered about her other passion – the seemingly unhappy love affair that Naomi had mentioned. Perhaps a married man? That was always an unhappy situation.

He said, 'Well, I'd like to buy some of your plants, when you're open for business. My garden needs them.'

'I promise to let you know.' She opened the door again for him. 'Where are you off to now, Colonel?'

'The Hall. It's my last stop.'

'It's a bit different from Naomi's day.'

'So I gather.'

'Shame it had to be turned into flats, though I gather they've been rather well done. Very luxurious. All the latest mod cons.'

'What are the residents like?'

'I've no idea. We never seem to see any of them around the village.'

'I was hoping they'd be both rich and generous.'

'Well, they must be fairly well-off because the flats cost a bit, from all accounts. Lois Delaney has taken one of them, apparently. The actress. I remember seeing her on the London stage years ago.'

'Yes, I saw her, too.' She had been one of the most beautiful actresses of her generation. A brunette with a heart-shaped face, emerald green eyes, perfect complexion and a wonderfully low, smoky voice. She belonged to the old and largely defunct school of glamorous glamour. It seemed to him that the leading young actresses of the present all looked rather ordinary and very much alike; he couldn't tell one from the other. The paparazzi snapped them arriving at airports in crumpled clothes and outsize sunglasses, and whenever they dressed up for some film première the result was usually a disastrous mess.

He said, 'I'm surprised Naomi didn't tell me.'

'I shouldn't think she knows. It doesn't seem to be on the general grapevine yet. I only heard because Tom Harvey was called out to see her the other day and he happened to mention it to me.'

She said it offhandedly but he saw a tell-tale blush begin in her cheeks. Ah-ha, he thought. Our nice young doctor is in with a chance.

He set off again, trudging through the snow. Ruth Swynford waved from the Manor doorstep and he waved back. It occurred to him, also, that the reason for Major Cuthbertson's miraculous recovery from flu and sudden desire to take over the collection had very probably been because he had also just heard the news of Lois Delaney. The colonel smiled to himself.

Three

'There's someone coming up the drive, Neville.'
'The postman?'
'No, not him. I don't think there's a delivery today. It's
a bloke, though.' Craig peered sideways through the
ground-floor window. 'He's going to the front door. Looks
like he's collecting for something. What'll I do?'
'Wait and see if he gets in. The Barnes's may not
open it.'
'S'posing they do? S'posing he comes here?'
Neville Avery looked at his lover with mild exasperation.
'You have two options, my dear Craig. Either you answer
the door, or you don't. In the first case, give the man some
money, in the second, do nothing and he'll go away. No
need to make a song and dance about it.'
The young man said sulkily, 'I'm not. I just wasn't sure
what you wanted me to do.'
He went on watching out of the window. The bloke
was still waiting for the door to be opened. A tall guy in
country tweeds with a posh look about him. The sort of
look that Neville had – though in a quite different way
– and which he himself would never have in a million
years, no matter how expensive the clothes he wore, or
how hard he tried. Whenever he saw himself in the mirror,
he realized that he still looked like what he had always
been: Craig Potter, born in Eltham, mother a barmaid,
father unknown, brought up with two brothers and a sister
(different fathers, unknown as well) in a two-room slum
that was also home to an army of cockroaches, mice and
bedbugs. At thirteen he had left – got out and headed for
the bright lights of the West End to seek his fortune. He'd

slept rough in doorways and under arches or in shelters for the homeless before he'd got a job in a restaurant kitchen, washing dishes and sweeping floors. Plenty of cockroaches and mice there, too, though the customers never knew it. Just as well people never saw what went on behind the swing doors or they'd never touch the nosh on their plates, let alone eat it. Blimey, he could tell some stories, even about the snobbiest places.

He'd worked as a skivvy for a few months, living in a hostel, before he'd moved on to a better place where he graduated from the sink to waiting at tables. He was rather good at it, being nimble on his feet and quick with his hands; he knew how to serve plates with a flourish and to whisk them away deftly, and he knew how to handle the customers. He bowed and scraped to the men, smiled charmingly at the women, flirted discreetly with the girls. It helped, too, that he wasn't a bad looker.

He had made several more moves to other kinds of restaurants – Italian, French, Greek, Spanish, picking up a smattering of whatever language was necessary. Because he was dark-haired and olive-skinned, he sometimes pretended to be the nationality of the restaurant, but it was risky. If a real French person, or a real Spaniard started gabbling away at him then he was made to look a fool and he didn't like that.

By the time he was seventeen, he was working in the very best places and it was at *Le Champignon Noir* that he had met Neville Avery, who had come in alone one lunchtime. There had been plenty of approaches from older men before but he'd never fancied the idea. It had been different with Neville, though. He'd come in several times before he'd said more to him than to give his order, but Craig had known very well that he was interested and he was flattered. He could tell that Neville was a genuine toff by the way he spoke and by the way he ate and by the way he behaved, and he'd obviously got plenty of dosh. Three or four months had gone by before he'd been invited to visit Neville's posh flat in Knightsbridge and, a month later, he'd chucked the waiting job and moved in. He'd settled into his new life quickly. Got used to being given money to spend on nice clothes, to being taken to the theatre and to swanky restaurants like the ones he'd slaved in before. Concerts and operas bored him stiff, but he sat through them somehow as part of the price. He might have got tired of it all eventually, except for two things: first, and much to his surprise, he'd fallen in love with Neville; and second, he'd learned to cook. Both those things had given meaning and purpose to his life and he was as near to being happy as he had ever been. At the back of his mind, though, lurked the fear that one day Neville would get fed up with him for being such an ignorant lowlife and throw him out.

The move to the country had worried him, but the doctor had said it was a good idea because of Neville's asthma and so he'd gone along with it. It was bloody dull after London, and he thought the Hall was an ugly old place, but he still had the cooking, and he still had Neville and sometimes he was allowed to help with making the dolls.

He'd been gobsmacked by the dolls, at first. It'd seemed such a weird thing for someone like Neville to do, and even weirder that so many people wanted to buy them and pay a fortune for them. But he had to admit that the dolls were ever so well done and ever so lifelike. Of course, they weren't made for children: they were what were called 'Collectors' Treasures' and a lot of them went to America where people fancied that sort of thing. Sometimes they were referred to in the barmy doll magazine advertisements as 'Heirlooms' or 'Keepsakes' and they were Limited Editions with their number on. Neville always signed his dolls in 22-carat gold.

The characters were either out of a film or a story book or they were real people – Snow White, Cinderella, Red Riding Hood, Alice in Wonderland, Her Majesty, the Queen, in her Coronation Robes and the Queen Mum in hers – that sort of thing – and Neville had done a very nice Angel of Glad Tidings specially for Christmas with green glass eyes, a velvet and gold braid robe, sparkling organza wings and holding a wooden lute. Craig's favourites were Scarlett O'Hara in the velvet green dress she'd made out of the curtains to visit Rhett Butler in prison and Grace Kelly in her lace wedding dress when she'd married Prince Rainier. He'd always thought Grace Kelly had real class.

Neville had someone to make the bisque porcelain heads and bodies but he did all the rest himself – hand painted the faces and hand set the eyes, glued on the real hair, made all the clothes, the shoes, the jewellery, the lot. It was fiddly work and took ages but Neville always said that every detail was important. Sometimes he let Craig do simple things, like sticking on sequins and stringing beads and Craig enjoyed it because it meant them working together. But he was really much better at cooking.

He'd once asked Neville why he bothered with the dolls; after all he didn't need the money when he'd got a stack of his own already. 'Because I enjoy it, dear boy,' had been the dry answer. 'And think of the pleasure I give to people.' Bloody odd people, Craig had thought to himself: playing about with dolls when they were grown-up. But of course he hadn't said so aloud.

The caretakers must have opened the door because the bloke had gone inside. Sure enough, after a moment or two, there was a ring at the flat door.

Neville said, 'You might as well answer it. 'Tis the season of goodwill to all men, after all.'

If it had been up to him he'd have pretended to be out, but it was like Neville to be generous. Craig opened the door. The bloke was even taller than he'd thought. He stood up very straight and the silver-grey hair looked what people always called 'distinguished'. His voice, when he spoke, matched the hair.

'So sorry to disturb you. I'm collecting for the Save the Donkey fund and wonder if you'd care to make a donation?'

Donkeys? Jesus, whatever next?

'Ask the gentleman in, Craig,' Neville called out. 'Don't leave him standing on the doorstep.'

There wasn't a proper doorstep, anyway, but he held the flat door open further and stood aside for the bloke to come in. Neville had got up from his table and was being ever so friendly.

'How do you do? I'm Neville Avery. Did I hear you say donkeys? I love the creatures. Amazing the way they have that cross on their backs, don't you think? I often wonder which came first – the cross or the Palm Sunday story.'

Neville was opening his wallet and feeding a note into the slit of the collecting tin – a tenner, Craig thought, by the look of it. What a waste! The bloke was thanking him ever so politely and he could see his glance wandering to the table and the doll that Neville was working on. Neville had noticed it too.

'My latest creation. The young Queen Victoria. What do you think of her?'

'Extraordinary. Did you do it all yourself?'

'Down to the last detail – except for the porcelain head and body. I have those specially fired for me. This portrays the moment when the princess has been awoken to be told that her uncle has died and that she is queen – hence the nightgown and the flowing locks. I've entitled it "I will be good".'

'Very apt.'

'Her own words, of course. Though she actually spoke them earlier on another occasion – when she first realized that she was the heir to the throne.'

After that, the bloke was shown other dolls and he admired those too. Or pretended to. It was hard to tell with someone like that. You never knew what they were thinking and they were much too polite to say if they thought something was crap. A lot of people thought the whole doll thing was a bit creepy, himself included. Anyway, Neville was telling the guy all about it and he was nodding away, as though he was really interested. He turned out to be Colonel something, which wasn't surprising. Neville beckoned him over.

'This is Craig, my companion.'

He'd never thought much of the word companion; it sounded like someone an old woman employed to run around after her. Partner would have been nicer but Neville never called him that.

The colonel's handshake made him wince and feel glad he'd never had to go into the army. All that marching up and down, and swinging from ropes and crawling through mud under barbed wire. He'd have hated it.

He was glad when the bloke finally pushed off with his donkey tin. He shut the door firmly behind him. Good riddance!

'I'm doing a mushroom risotto for lunch, Neville, and I thought we'd have a tomato salad to go with it. Will that suit?'

'Whatever you like, dear boy. You always produce something delicious.'

He went off into the kitchen and got busy.

The caretaker who had let the colonel into the Hall had mentioned that Lois Delaney lived in Flat 2 on the ground floor.

'The famous actress, sir. She came here to get away from it all. I expect when you're famous like her, people bother you all the time.'

The colonel rather doubted that the younger generation would be interested enough, but there were still plenty of older fans who might pester her. He wondered what the protocol was with famous celebrities in hiding. Did you pretend not to recognize them, or would that offend them even more than being pestered? In the event, when he pressed the bell of the second ground-floor flat, nobody answered. Rather disappointing.

The caretaker, who apparently lived with his wife on the ground floor at the back, had also offered the information that there were three more smaller flats on the first floor and a further one above, in the attics. The colonel made his way up a fine oak staircase illuminated by a large and luridly-coloured stained glass window. As Naomi had admitted, the Hall was a bit of a Victorian horror – outside and in – but it had all the good qualities of its era. It was very well built, spacious and solid.

He pressed the bell of the nearest of the first-floor flats and it was answered by a man about the same age as himself. Not ex-service, though. Judging by the faintly yellow hue to his complexion, he had retired from some post involving many years spent under a tropical sun. A contribution was duly given – several pound coins clinking into the tin.

'Sorry it isn't more. My wife usually has plenty of change but she's away at the moment. You're local, I expect?'

'A mere newcomer,' the colonel said. 'I only moved to Frog End last year.'

'Army?'

'How did you guess?'

'You can always tell an old soldier. For one thing they always stand up straight. It's a bit early, but can I offer you a New Year drink?'

He was shown in to a large and pleasant room with windows overlooking the back of the house. He had been right about the tropics.

The large ebony elephant standing in one corner; the jade dragons breathing fire on the mantelpiece; the heavily carved hardwood furniture and rattan chairs; the paintings of waxen flowers, lush palms and distant mountain peaks; and a framed photograph of a verandaed bungalow very different from those he had just visited – they were all from the Far East.

It was his turn to make a guess. 'Malaya?'

'That's right. My wife and I spent more than thirty years out there. I was in the import/export business and we moved around quite a bit: Penang and Kuala Lumpur and Singapore. We only came back to England a few months ago. The name's Ward – Roy Ward.'

The colonel introduced himself and they shook hands. He was handed a glass of very pale sherry.

'How do you like being back here?'

'To be perfectly frank, I hate it. I'd have stayed on out

in Malaya for ever but my wife wanted to get home to be near her family. We've a daughter and son both living over here, and there's Jean's sister, too. She's just had a hip operation and Jean's gone to look after her. So, I'm stuck here wishing I wasn't.'

The colonel sympathized. He, too, had found it very hard to settle down in England after serving all over the world.

'Yes, it takes some getting used to again.'

They talked about Malaya and Singapore for a while and places that they had both known – the Cricket Club, Tanglin, Raffles, the sailing club, the racecourse, beaches, hill stations, the impenetrable jungle that had been supposed to keep the Japanese army out.

Roy Ward said, 'We should never have lost Singapore to the Japs. It was a complete fiasco.'

The colonel agreed. Who could not? 'Not something the British Army can be proud of.'

'In fact, the writing was on the wall for the British decades ago – well before 1942 – and it has to be said that, on the whole, we got pretty much what we deserved. Yes, the British turned Singapore Island from swamp and jungle into one of the world's greatest trading places, but we feathered our own nests at the same time and lived like lords. It couldn't last for ever, though. When I went out there in the early Sixties there were still remnants of the old colonial life and it was good while it lasted. Servants and sunshine and an endless round of pleasure. Not quite so wonderful for the natives, of course. But I loved everything about Malaya. The good, the bad and the ugly.'

'Even the mosquitoes?'

'Well, you get used to them, don't you? And the snakes and the spiders and the scorpions and all the rest. You learn to live with them. They never worried me.'

The colonel said drily, 'Frog End must seem a bit on the quiet side.'

'It certainly does.'

'But you have a resident celebrity at the Hall to liven things up: Lois Delaney.'

'Yes, she has a flat downstairs but we never see her. Did you meet her just now?'

'Unfortunately not. I'm a big fan but she didn't answer the door.'

'As a matter of fact, I came across her many years ago when I first when out to Singapore – before I met Jean.'

'Oh?'

'She was touring in *Blithe Spirit* and there was a big party given at Raffles after the performance for the company. I had happened to be invited. Somebody played a piano and she sang several Coward songs.'

'I didn't realize she could sing.'

'Oh yes, she was very good. It was quite an evening. I'll never forget it.'

'Did you actually meet her?'

'Yes. I saw quite a bit of her while she was in Singapore.'

'What was she like?'

Roy Ward said, 'Delightful. Charming.' He added quietly, 'The most beautiful woman I ever saw.'

How many other men, the colonel wondered – himself included – had thought exactly the same thing?

He finished the excellent sherry and Roy Ward saw him to the door.

'You must come and have another drink when Jean gets back.'

'Thank you, I'd like that.'

'Where do you live?'

'Pond Cottage. It's by the green. Do call in any time you're passing.'

He proceeded to the next flat and pressed the bell. As he waited, a door at the end of the corridor opened.

'They're away. Gone abroad. Who let you in?'

'The caretaker.'

'He's not supposed to. It's against our security rules.'

The woman came closer. She was a type he had come across before. A woman of an age even more uncertain than Lois Delaney's but who had never ever been remotely beautiful. Her grey hair was waved in corrugated iron ridges, and she had a thin and bloodless mouth. Her resentment of the poor hand life had dealt her was written in her face. She would be carping, critical, bitter, and often trouble-making.

'I'm very sorry to have disturbed you,' he said. 'I'm collecting for a charity.'

'I don't give to charities. It all gets spent on the people who run them.'

'Then I won't trouble you any further, madam,' he said politely. He turned away and she called after him.

'They should never have let you in.'

A narrower flight of stairs went on up to the attics. In Naomi's childhood days this would have led to the servants' bedrooms – dormer-windowed rooms with cheap lino floors, iron bedsteads, pine washstands, china ewers and bowls. There might have been rag rugs, thin cotton curtains, a patchwork cushion, perhaps a framed sample of wool cross-stitch: *Thou God Seest Me.*

He pressed the bell beside the door, which was opened by a girl – no thin-lipped grey gorgon this time, thank goodness. She was somewhere in her early thirties, he reckoned, and so still a girl to him. Her hair was chestnut-coloured and long – worn twisted up in a careless, wispy knot on the top of her head and secured with a tortoiseshell clip. She was dressed in jeans and some kind of loose smock. Once again, he apologized for intruding.

She put her head on one side. 'Donkeys? Goodness, that's a new one.'

'They need saving. Some people treat them very badly. It's a good cause.'

She smiled. 'I'm sure it is. And I rather like them. Come in while I find some money.'

He followed her into a long room that was obviously being used as a studio. One end was taken up with a trestle table, easel, paints, brushes – all the clutter of an artist. The rest of the room was furnished with a very modern sofa, equally modern chairs and a coffee table. Not to his taste but he knew that he was hopelessly old-fashioned.

'They knocked three poky rooms into one,' she said, seeing him looking round. 'Rather a good idea, really, and it was just what I wanted for work.'

He glanced with interest towards the trestle table. 'What sort of work do you do?'

'I paint plates. Come and see. I'm doing one at the moment.'

He looked down at the china plate and the delicate painting of two goldfinches perched on the branches of some flowering shrub.

'It's not finished yet,' she said. 'And it'll have a gold rim, to set it off. It's called "Golden Song". I specialize in birds and flowers but I do other commissions, too. Commemorative plates, birth plates, wedding plates, christening plates . . . all that sort of stuff. As long as people pay, I do it.'

First, the dolls downstairs and now this, he thought. There must be something about the house.

'It's beautifully painted,' he said – which, indeed, it was.

'Thank you. I hate the plates, to be honest, but the punters love them. Did you come across Neville and his dolls downstairs?'

'Yes, indeed.'

'He tipped me off about the US market. It's a gold mine. Americans love collecting things like this and they pay very good money.' She waved a hand towards some canvases stacked against the walls – not pretty birds and blossoms but bold, modern splashes of colour. 'That's my real work, but, of course, it doesn't sell anything like as well and I have to earn a living.'

She fed some coins into the tin and he handed her a donkey badge.

'Thank you very much.'

She let him out of the flat door. 'Happy New Year.'

He'd almost forgotten about it. 'And to you.'

'Jeanette's the name. Jeanette Hayes.'

He told her his.

She looked at him curiously. 'I don't think I've ever met

a real live colonel before. Never moved in those sort of circles.'

'We're quite normal,' he said, smiling. 'At least, I hope so.'

A woman was waiting in the hall at the foot of the stairs – he saw her as he turned the corner of the last flight: a dumpy figure in a flowered overall, one hand gripping the newel post and staring up at him.

'You must be the gentleman Stanley let in to do the collecting.'

'That's right,' he said, hoping there wasn't going to be any trouble.

'I'm Mrs Barnes. My husband and me are caretakers here. I was wondering if you'd got any answer from Miss Delaney in Flat Two?'

'No, I'm afraid I didn't. Perhaps she's away?'

She shook her head. 'No, she's not. She can't be. She was here yesterday evening and she always tells us if she's going away so we can keep an eye on things. I'm a bit worried, sir, to tell you the truth. I rang her bell a few times earlier this morning to see if she wanted me to come and give the flat a bit of a tidy-up for her. It's hard to get any cleaning help round here, so I've been going in twice a week to see to things.'

'Well, perhaps she's gone out?'

'No, she hasn't. Her car's there and it hasn't been moved – you can tell because of the snow. I was wondering if something had happened . . . whether I should open the door?'

'You have a spare key?'

'Yes, sir. Me and Stanley keep keys to all the flats – so we can get in if anything goes wrong. Water leaks, or power failures, or something like that. But, of course, we wouldn't dream of entering unless we felt the matter was urgent.'

'No, I'm sure you wouldn't,' he said soothingly. 'Supposing you ring the bell once again, and, if there's still no answer, you could take a look – just to make sure all's well.'

'Would you mind accompanying me, sir?'

He was often called upon to do something authoritative. It was the 'colonel' bit, he assumed. People looked to him to decide what was the best action to take. But, in this particular case, he really had no idea. Lois Delaney might have an overnight male visitor, or she might be nursing a thumping New Year hangover, or she might simply not wish to be disturbed. In any of those cases, she was going to be far from pleased at somebody invading her privacy. On the other hand, Mrs Barnes seemed genuinely worried and she did not seem the excitable type.

He went with her to the door of Flat 2 and stood by while she produced a key from her pocket and fitted it into the lock. He fully expected a security chain to hold the door but, instead, it opened freely and Mrs Barnes poked her head inside and called out.

'Miss Delaney . . . excuse me, but are you all right? Miss Delaney?'

There was no answer. The light was out in the hallway, and in the kitchen near the door and when they advanced into the sitting room, it was in darkness, too – the curtains still drawn across the windows. The scent of some expensive French scent lingered on the air. The colonel found a light switch and clicked it on but nothing happened. He tried another switch with the same result.

'I think the fuses must have blown, Mrs Barnes. Do the flats have their own electricity circuits?'

'Yes, sir. They're wired separately, with their own meters.'

'Have you got a torch?'

'I'll fetch one, sir.'

She was back in a moment and he took the torch from her – a heavy-duty affair with a powerful beam. He shone it around the room, illuminating pale silk upholstery, tasselled cushions, fringed lamps, glass tables, gilt-edged mirrors, a plethora of silver-framed studio portraits. A star's room, if ever there was one.

'The bedroom's next door.' Mrs Barnes had spoken in a church whisper. 'Should we go in?'

'I think we'd better.'

She knocked at the closed door and then opened it. The room was also dark and the torch showed that the shiny peach bedcover and the arrangement of matching cushions were undisturbed. The French scent was overlaid now by a more pungent one of pine.

'Is that a bathroom through there?'

Mrs Barnes nodded. 'Do you mind looking, sir?'

The bathroom door was ajar and, by the torchlight, the colonel saw the plastic-covered electrical cord snaking in through the gap from a power point in the bedroom skirting board.

He said in the tone he had used to issue army commands that needed to be obeyed without question, 'Stay exactly where you are, Mrs Barnes. Don't move and, whatever you do, don't touch anything.'

He pushed the door further open with his booted foot and shone the torch inside.

Lois Delaney was lying naked in the bath to the left of the doorway. She was facing him, her head and shoulders above the water, the rest of her body beneath. He saw at once that she was dead and the obvious cause of her death – an electric hairdryer – was submerged beside her body, its cord caught up on her big toe. Her eyes, shining like emeralds in the torchlight, were wide with surprise, her mouth a little open.

He said crisply, over his shoulder, 'Go and call the police, Mrs Barnes. Quick as you can. Tell them Miss Delaney has been found dead.'

She gave a shriek of horror. 'Oh, my God! Oh, my God! What a terrible thing to happen! Oh, my God!'

'Do what I said, Mrs Barnes. At once.'

He waited alone with the dead actress. He would have liked to cover her nakedness for the sake of her dignity but nothing could be done for her, nothing touched, nothing moved. The water looked greenish and smelled strongly of the pine bath essence that she must have tipped in from a big glass bottle up on a shelf.

Her half-open mouth looked for all the world as though it was about to speak to him. To tell him something. But, of course, it couldn't. Tragic to think that the gloriously husky voice would never be heard again. He turned the torch away from the bath.

He had remembered the third silent thing now.

The falling snow . . . the hour before the dawn . . . the mouth of one just dead.

Four

'We've met before, haven't we, sir? The case of Lady Swynford.'

The colonel rose slowly to his feet. 'Yes, indeed.'

Detective Inspector Squibb of the Dorset Police looked as natty as ever – sharp grey suit, gleaming white shirt, silk tie, trendy haircut. No particular accent from no particular place.

'You remember Detective Sergeant Biddlecombe?'

He nodded. 'Certainly.'

The sergeant was much older than his superior – ruddy-faced and rumpled, with a rich Dorset burr. Chalk and cheese.

Squibb said, 'I'd like a few words with you, sir, if you don't mind. Before you'll be permitted to leave the Hall.'

'Of course.'

Mrs Barnes, still very shocked and upset, had been allowed go and lie down while the police carried out their work, and the colonel had waited patiently in the sitting area at the far end of the hall in front of a vast stone fireplace. The other residents had been peremptorily ordered to stay in their flats. Eventually, Lois Delaney's body had been removed on a trolley.

They sat down and the police sergeant produced his notepad and clicked his biro into action.

Inspector Squibb picked up the Save the Donkey tin from the table and looked at the picture. 'You were collecting for this charity, then, sir? Not one I've ever heard of, I'm bound to say.'

The colonel didn't care for the faint smirk that went

with the remark. 'The prevention of mindless cruelty to animals is a fairly worthwhile cause, as I'm sure you'll agree.'

'Oh, of course, sir.'

The smirk vanished and the questions started. What time had he arrived at the Hall? Which flats had he called at? Who had he spoken to? Who had he seen? How had he come to discover the body? He controlled his irritation at the brusque and rather accusing manner in which they were asked. He described how Mrs Barnes had been worried about Miss Delaney and had asked him to go with her into Flat 2, which had been in darkness with none of the lights working. How Mrs Barnes had fetched a torch. How he had shone it into the bathroom and seen Miss Delaney lying in the bath. How it had been very clear that she was dead. As he spoke, the electric logs on the fireplace hearth were flickering away merrily.

'Did either of you touch or move anything?'

'Only the doors. Mrs Barnes opened the entrance door and the one to the bedroom. The bathroom door was slightly ajar and I opened that with my boot.'

'Very wise, considering.'

'Yes, I'd noticed the electric lead. Then I saw the hairdryer in the bath. She had obviously been electrocuted.'

'An accident, you thought?'

'Hardly. Nobody in their right mind would use or touch anything live while taking a bath. Either she had done it deliberately herself, or somebody else had.'

'But you hadn't seen anybody about the Hall or in the grounds? A visitor, a stranger?'

'No. Nobody.'

'Have you ever been here before?'

'No, never.'

'You're not acquainted with any of the residents?'

'No. I'd never met any of them.'

'You didn't know the deceased, then?'

'Only by reputation. She was a very well-known actress, of course. I'd seen her on the London stage, but I'd never met her in person. I wasn't aware that she was living at the

Hall until this morning. I don't believe it was common knowledge in the village.'

'A bit past it, wasn't she, sir? Over the hill.'

He wished more than ever that Lois Delaney had not been exposed to the merciless eyes of the police: the dyed hair, the crow's feet, the jaw line sagging, the body no longer firm.

He said coldly, 'She was still a very beautiful woman.'

Another faint smirk, or had he simply imagined it? In any case, it was pointless defending her to this cocky young man whose idea of female beauty would be something very different from his own.

'Well, thank you, sir. That will be all – for the moment. I'll be interviewing all the residents, as well as Mr and Mrs Barnes. I take it that you'll be staying in Frog End for the next few days? You'll be required to attend the inquest, of course, and you may be needed for further questioning.'

'I have no plans to go away.'

The inspector stood up. 'Don't go making a habit of it, will you, sir?'

'A habit of what, Inspector?'

'Finding dead bodies.'

He hadn't imagined the smirk this time.

He walked back through the snow to Pond Cottage and left the collection tin and the badges on the hall table. Later on, he would take them over to Miss Butler across the green; for the moment, he felt in need of a stiff drink. Thursday, who had re-established himself at the end of the sofa, opened his yellow eyes as he went into the sitting room and then shut them again. The colonel lit the log fire, poured himself a neat whisky and sat down in his wing-back tapestry chair.

What a sad business! A woman like Lois Delaney to end her life so ignominiously. He could vaguely remember some other case of another woman celebrity – a TV personality – killing herself in the same way, only it had been with an electric fire, not a hairdryer. Murder seemed most unlikely, on the face of it. The murderer would have had to run a bath, persuade the victim to undress, get in and stay there obediently while the hairdryer was fetched, switched on and chucked into the water. Rather far fetched, to say the least.

And yet he couldn't forget the half-open mouth, the lips parted as though she had wanted to speak to him – if only she could. The third and most silent thing of all – *the mouth of one just dead*.

Somehow Lois Delaney had not looked as though she had wanted to die; on the contrary, he had the strongest feeling that she had wanted to live. He shook his head and downed some more whisky. He was definitely getting over-fanciful in his old age.

'You never told me you knew her, Neville.'

'I don't tell you everything that's ever happened in my life, Craig, dear boy. There isn't time. I came across her in my costume design days. As I recall, I did her dresses for *Blithe Spirit* and one of those Rattigan plays – *French Without Tears*, I think.'

Another thing kept from him. He pouted. 'I didn't know you did theatre costumes.'

'Many moons ago. I was rather good but I got bored with it. Theatre folk can be very tiresome to deal with. All ego and tantrums. I prefer the dolls – they wear what I make for them and don't argue or create any dramas – though Lois Delaney was rather sweet, actually, and quite lovely.'

'Did you know she was living here?'

'As it happens, I did. Mrs Barnes told me.'

'Did you go to her flat?'

'No, I didn't. I very much doubt if Lois would have remembered me. As I said, it was a long time ago. A great deal of water has flowed under the bridge since then.'

'She was old as the hills, wasn't she?'

'To you, yes. Not to me. You're looking jealous again, Craig. No need to be. You're rather nice-looking, too. And you know quite well that much as I admire beautiful women, that's as far as it goes with me.'

'I didn't like that policeman. He'd got a cheek, asking all those stupid questions.'

'It's his job, dear boy. Don't take it so personally.'

'Well, I didn't like the way he looked at us.'

'You should be used to it by now.'

Craig knew that he should, but it always pissed him off when people gave him and Neville looks. Sometimes they were sort of knowing leers; sometimes they were cold and disapproving; other times they were downright disgusted. Well, gays had rights like anybody else. There was a law that said you couldn't be against them. And about time, too. They'd had to fight for it – demos and marches and bracelets and all the rest – but they'd done it. Funny how you could nearly always spot another gay and some of them – like Neville – didn't really look it at all. But you *knew*.

He said, 'Do you think she topped herself?'

'Presumably. One doesn't normally use a hairdryer in the bath. Not if one has any sense. Mind you, the acting profession isn't exactly the most sensible on the planet. I expect she was depressed about something – they're either on cloud nine or down in the dumps. And it's true her star was waning. Well, waned actually, to be brutally frank. Always a hard thing to accept, especially when you're on your own with nobody to hold your hand.'

'Didn't she have a bloke? A husband?'

'She'd had three. The latest was a very rich property tycoon but they were separated, I believe. It was his company that converted this place into flats. Or *one* of his companies, I should say. He seems to have fingers in several different pies.'

'How do you know all that?'

'It's in the newspapers, dear boy – even the broadsheets. They muck-rake along with the rest these days. You really should read more.'

Craig hardly ever read anything, except for cooking recipes and even then he mostly made them up himself. He thought people who followed every word of a recipe and measured and weighed everything were pathetic. Real

cooking wasn't like that. Real cooking was trying things
out, chucking things in, tasting till you got it right and
knowing when you had.

He went to the window and looked out. It was still
odd that Neville hadn't ever mentioned knowing that
actress. She was pretty famous, after all, even though
she was old hat, and Neville was always dropping names.
Casual, like. Mind-blowing the number of celebs he seemed
to know.

He drummed his fingers on the window pane. Neville
hadn't given a toss but that cop had really got up his nose
with all his questions. Had they seen any strangers in or
around the house? Had they heard anything? Had they been
in all the evening? He'd kept quiet then because Neville
had left the flat for a while. His work lamp had been playing
up, going on and off, and he'd taken it to see Mr B and
ask if he could fix it. Matter of fact, he'd been gone quite
a long time. Not that Craig was going to tell that bastard
Squibb. He hated cops. They used to come round and worry
the life out of Mum about what his two brothers and he
had been up to. And he'd lost count of the number of times
he'd been picked-on in the street. Victimization, that's what
it'd been. Harassment. Catch him helping them with their
sodding inquiries now!

That colonel bloke was coming up the drive again – no
donkey tin this time, though. What the hell did he want
now?

'I'm so sorry to disturb you, Mrs Barnes. I'm afraid I left
my gloves behind. I think they're probably on the table by
the hall fireplace.'

'Come in, sir. I'll go and look straight away.'

He waited on the mat by front door while she hurried
off, snow melting off his boots in the warmth of very effi-
cient central heating. She still looked upset, he thought.
Still in shock, probably. He hoped Detective Inspector
Squibb had been considerate to her, though it seemed
unlikely. She came back with his leather gloves and he
thanked her.

'Stupid of me to go off without them.'

'I'm always losing mine,' she said. 'It's easy to do.'

He smiled at her. 'I hope you're feeling a bit better today.'

She shook her head. 'Not really, sir. It's been such a shock. I was ever so fond of Miss Delaney. She was such a nice lady. Always please and thank you, ever so grateful for anything you did. Not like some. My husband thought the world of her, too. We used to worry about her – being on her own. Of course, she went to London quite often to the hairdresser and to do some shopping and to stay with friends, but it must have been lonely for her down here.'

He said gently, 'I'm sure you were a great help to her.'

'We did what we could. I kept things tidy – she wasn't very good at that – and I gave the place a good clean every so often. And Stanley did odd jobs and any heavy stuff – moving furniture around, changing bulbs, mending things and suchlike. She was always moving furniture. Women are like that, aren't they?'

Laura had been, he remembered. Sometimes he'd come home to find a room completely rearranged. Men generally preferred everything to stay the same for ever. Something to do with habit and routine.

He said, 'Had Miss Delaney seemed at all depressed lately?'

'The inspector asked me that too, sir. The fact is that you never knew what sort of mood she'd be in. Sometimes when I'd go in, she was all smiles, then the next I could tell she was all unhappy. She was up and down, you see.' Mrs Barnes twisted her hands. 'I shouldn't say this about her now she's passed away, but she used to drink a bit – well, more than a bit, to tell the truth. It was always vodka. Vodka and tomato juice with some Worcestershire sauce. That's what she liked. She kept a big jug of it mixed up in the fridge so it was nice and cold.'

'Bloody Mary.'

'Beg pardon, sir?'

'That's what that particular drink is called. A Bloody Mary.'

'Well, I used to think that at least the tomato juice would be doing her some good because she didn't eat much else. Just snacks, really. No wonder she was so slim.'

'Was she here over Christmas?'

'Oh yes, sir. Her son, Mr Farrell, came to stay. He seemed a very nice gentleman but, of course, we only had a few words. Ever so good-looking. A lot like her. He's an actor, too. I've seen him once or twice on television – only in small parts, but you notice him, if you know what I mean.'

'Did he stay long?'

'Till New Year's Eve. Well, not the evening exactly. He left before lunchtime, I believe. Around midday. I didn't see him go myself, but Stanley did. He was outside getting in the logs when Mr Farrell drove away. He had one of those old sports cars.'

'So Miss Delaney was on her own after that?'

'No, sir. Her husband came to see her. Well, he's not really her husband any more. They were separated about three months ago. That's what Miss Delaney told me. She said the divorce settlement hadn't been finalized yet and so she'd come here for the time being. It was her husband's company that had converted the Hall into flats, you see. Flat Two hadn't been sold yet so it came in handy while she was waiting for things to be worked out. It can take months and months with a divorce, she told me, especially if there's a lot of money involved. She said the lawyers argue over every penny and they make a fortune themselves.'

He smiled. 'I dare say she was right. Did you tell the inspector all this?'

'Yes, sir. He asked lots of questions and I answered them. He wanted to know what time Miss Delaney's husband had arrived and when he left. Well, I could tell him that all right because Mr King couldn't get any answer when he pressed the outside bell to Miss Delaney's flat. All the flats have a numbered bell by the front door you see, sir. You have to speak into a sort of grille and say who you are, then the person in the flat presses a button to open the front door to let you in. Only she didn't. So, in the end he rang our bell – like you just now, sir – and I opened the front door for him.'

'You knew who he was?'

'Oh, yes. He'd interviewed us personally for the care-takers' job. He was very particular about the people he employed on his properties. Very particular about every-thing, come to that. He used to come here when the house was being converted and give the workmen a real telling-off if he found out things weren't being done properly.'

'I don't expect he was too pleased that the doorbell wasn't working.'

'He certainly wasn't, sir!'

'What sort of time was that?'

'As I told the inspector, it must have been about a quarter past five. It was dark, of course, and it was snowing quite hard. I remember that.'

'Did Mr King stay long?'

'No. And I know exactly when he left because he came and rang at our door when he was going. Stanley had just sat down to watch the BBC six o'clock news on the television and he had to get up again. Mr King ticked him off about the bell not working properly. He told Stanley he was to get it fixed immediately. We both saw him out of the front door and he drove off in that big car of his.'

'So he must have been the last person to see Mrs Delaney alive?'

She shook her head. 'No, sir. That was me. Well, I didn't actually *see* her, but I heard her. After Miss Delaney's husband had gone I rang her flat doorbell – just to make sure she was all right. I thought she might have been a bit upset, what with the divorce proceedings and Mr King visiting. She didn't open the door – just called through it, but she sounded quite all right. Everything was fine, she said, and she was just running her bath. She generally took a bath about that time in the evening if she was at home. Had a nice long soak with lots of Wiberg's pine essence in it. She always laughed and said it was very old-fashioned these days but it helped her relax. So, I didn't worry any more. Not till the next day when she didn't answer.'

He said sympathetically, 'This must have been very distressing for you, Mrs Barnes.'

'It has, sir. And the inspector says I'll have to give evidence at the inquest. He says I'll be asked the same sort of questions all over again. I'm dreading that, sir.'

He put a hand on her shoulder. 'There's nothing to worry about, Mrs Barnes. Just tell them the truth.'

'The truth, the whole truth and nothing but the truth . . . isn't that what I'll have to swear to tell, sir? I've seen it on the TV.'

'That's right,' he said. 'And it's all you have to do.'

'I saw you. You didn't know someone was watching, did you?'

The malevolent hiss came from behind her as she reached the landing from the attic stairs. Jeanette looked over her shoulder. That sour old biddy, Miss Quinn, was standing a few feet away. When she had first moved in to the Hall she had wondered what someone like Miss Quinn did all day; then she had found out. The woman spent her days spying on everybody else. A door had only to open or shut, a visitor arrive or leave, and she was out of her lair like a jack-in-the-box and peering over banisters, down, or up, to see what was going on.

'Is there something the matter, Miss Quinn?'

'I saw you.'

'And you can see me now.'

'I saw you standing outside her door last evening.'

'Whose door?'

'That actress. The one who's just died. What were you doing there, I'd like to know?'

'I really think, Miss Quinn, that your New Year's resolution should be to keep your long nose out of everybody else's business.'

She went on down the next flight of stairs to the hall and let herself out of the front door. It was bitterly cold after the warmth of the house and she wound her woollen scarf closer round her neck and hunched into her coat collar. What a damned nuisance that the old girl had spotted her! She was bound to have told the police. Of course, they may or may not have believed her – they must come across sad people like Miss Quinn all the time – but the probability was that they would ask if it was true. They would also ask her why she hadn't mentioned it to them before. Damn, damn, damn.

She walked on down the drive, heading for nowhere – just walking to get out of the flat and do some thinking. In a better mood she would have appreciated the wintry scene – the deep and crisp snow, the crimson sun sinking behind the woods, the stark black tracery of the leafless trees. But not right now.

She trod in the tyre tracks on the driveway – the police car's, presumably. There were footprints, too, alongside the tyre marks – large booted ones which would belong to that nice colonel who had come to collect money for the donkeys and who had found Lois. Poor man, it must have been horrible, though he had probably seen a good many dead bodies in his army days.

She reached the gates – hideous new shiny green ones, topped with lacquered brass balls. On the outside of one of the pillars an equally hideous square of slate had been let into the brickwork with *The Hall* engraved in fake Gothic script. She wondered what the former owners made of it all. Not that the conversion had been shoddily done. Far from it. The driveway and the grounds were immaculate, and no expense had been spared on the interior. Everything was top quality and everything worked. She couldn't complain about any of it. And the village itself, of course, was lovely. She'd come here to get some peace and Dorset had seemed a very good place to get it. It was just rotten luck that Lois should have moved in and then, of course, Rex had turned up again like a bad penny, blast him! And just when she was beginning to get over the bastard.

She walked on along the empty road. The rooks were wheeling and cawing above the dark woods, settling down for the night. Not much of an inspiration for the painted plates with their sweet song-birds and delicate flowers. Sometimes she got so sick of the plates she wanted to hurl them across the room – smash them into tiny pieces. Only she couldn't do that. They made money. Income. Her inheritance had paid for the flat and she knew it had been a sound investment: easy to keep up, easy to sell when she wanted to move on, ideal to work in. Far better and more sensible than buying some dank, dark, poky, dry-rot-ridden cottage. But she still had to eat. She had to keep doing the plates, whether she liked them or not.

After half a mile or so she turned back. It was getting darker and starting to snow again.

'You're not thinking of going out, I hope, Roger?'

The major started guiltily – caught in the act of putting on his coat and scarf. Marjorie was standing behind him in the hallway, hands on her hips.

'Just thought I'd take a turn. Get some fresh air into the old lungs.'

'Get pneumonia, you mean. If you've got flu, you should stay indoors.'

'Matter of fact, I'm feeling much more the thing now. All tickety-boo again.'

'Is that so? You're still not going out, though. It's snowing again and it's getting dark.'

'Really? I hadn't noticed.'

'Yes, you had, Roger. I can read you like a book, you know. You were planning to walk over to the Hall and see if you could somehow get to meet that actress.'

'What actress?'

'Don't put on that innocent look. Lois Delaney. The one you were always so keen on.'

'Nothing was further from my mind, I assure you.'

'That's just as well, then, because she's not there any more.'

'What do you mean? Not there any more?'

'She's not there any more because she was found dead this morning and they've taken her away.'

He gaped at his wife. '*Dead? Lois Delaney?*'

'That's what I said. You must be going deaf, Roger. You ought to go and see Dr Harvey about it. Perhaps you need a hearing aid.'

A hearing aid! What did she think he was? An old man? He clutched at the coat stand, feeling damned shaky all of a sudden. It was the shock, of course. Hearing bad news like that, and from Marjorie who didn't care how she delivered it. Tact wasn't exactly her middle name.

He said, 'Are you quite sure?'

'Of course I'm sure. It's all round the village. The police have been at the Hall and they went to the colonel's cottage to question him.'

'*The colonel!*'

'I wish you wouldn't keep repeating what I say, like a parrot. The colonel was the one who found her body – when he was collecting for the donkey fund.'

'You mean he went into her flat?'

'Well, he must have done because she died in the bath. They think it was suicide.'

Major Cuthbertson's mind was reeling as he tried to make sense of it. The colonel had got into the flat – just as he'd feared – in which case Lois Delaney must have let him in. So why had she then got into a bath and killed herself? What the hell had gone on? He wiped his brow.

Steady the guns! Rally the troops! Don't let the old girl see how fussed you are.

'You said the colonel found her?'

'Yes, Roger, I did. The caretaker's wife was worried because she couldn't get any answer at the flat and she asked the colonel to go in and see if anything was wrong. So he did. And he found Lois Delaney dead in the bath.'

'That's shocking!'

'It was for her – she'd been electrocuted.'

'Good God!'

'Lucky it wasn't you who found her, Roger. You'd probably have had a heart attack and fallen in the bath as well.'

He let go of the coat rack and drew himself up, squaring his shoulders. 'I don't find that very amusing.'

'It wasn't meant to be.' Marjorie was looking at him with one of her narrow-eyed expressions – the kind she wore when she'd smelled some sort of rat. 'Did you already know she was living at the Hall – *before* I told you?'

'Certainly not.'

'Because it would be just like you to have gone round hot foot and pestered her. Got yourself involved in it all. Then we'd have the police coming round to question *you*.'

'What an absurd idea!'

'No, it isn't. Remember what a fool you made of yourself over Ursula Swynford before she was murdered? How she played you along like a fish on a line and made fun of you behind your back? I even wondered for a while if you might have killed her in a rage, till I decided you weren't capable of it. Not *you*, Roger.'

This was not a compliment, he realized. Far from it. He took off his scarf and coat and hung them carefully back on the rack.

'Matter of fact, I don't feel as good as I thought. The old pins are a bit wobbly. I think I'll go and sit down and take it easy for a bit.'

'Yes, I should do that, if I were you. We don't want your flu coming back again.'

He went into the living room and made straight for the cocktail bar, not caring if Marjorie heard him or not. *Drink To Me Only With Thine Eyes* had reached the end of the first verse by the time his shaky hand had extracted the whisky bottle and poured an extra stiff one.

He sat down in the chair beside the electric fire, his mind still going round in circles. Good God, what a thing to happen! And to think he might have got mixed up in it! Just like he'd been when Ursula had been murdered. Marjorie didn't know the half of that, of course. She'd no idea that he'd gone up to Ursula's bedroom and found her dead on the bed – just like the colonel had found Lois Delaney. Well, not quite like that. Lois Delaney had been in the bath, not on the bed – which presumably meant she'd had no clothes on. In the buff! That was shocking, too. Call him old-fashioned but it seemed a damned undignified way to go, especially for a lady like her. The colonel would have felt exactly the same – no doubt about that. They'd stand shoulder-to-shoulder on it. Dammit, they were both gentlemen. Men of the world. Appalling thing to happen. Such a beautiful woman! Such a shame!

The major took another large gulp of whisky and shook his head sadly.

Five

The obituary in the newspaper took up nearly the whole page and carried a large photograph of Lois Delaney, obviously taken some years ago. Her chin was resting lightly on one slender hand, her head tilted at a slight angle, her hair a soft dark cloud framing her heart-shaped face and her lips parted in a smile. The colonel found his eyes drawn to that mouth: the same mouth that he had seen in very different circumstances.

He started to read the obituary with interest. She had been born in exactly the same year as himself, which made her considerably older than he had thought. It was clear that she had come from a well-to-do family – father vaguely described as holding directorships, mother the younger daughter of a baronet. She had attended a select private boarding school in Hampshire then gone, not through the grinding mill of RADA or the Central, but straight on to the stage in a junior role in some now-forgotten drawing-room comedy. From there on, she had never looked back. At twenty-one, she had been married a naval officer, Lieutenant Charles Roper. Marriage dissolved less than two years later, so clearly a mistake.

Her steady rise to fame was charted through the many parts she had played. Not heavily dramatic roles with moral messages but ones that had appealed to the legions of theatregoers simply wanting to be entertained and which had showed off all her style and her glamour, as well as her husky voice, to perfection. She had married for the second time, ten years after the first: an actor, Ian Farrell, who had been her leading man on several occasions but who was barely remembered now. That marriage had lasted longer – almost eight years – before it, too, had been dissolved. There had been one son, Rex.

The starring parts had dwindled gradually as trends and times had changed. There had been a few cameo roles in various television series, a supporting part in a film, and then, finally, she had married Bruce King, a wealthy property developer. She had made a reappearance on the West End stage but the play in question had folded after only a few weeks and she had, apparently, retired from acting. She had recently separated from her third husband. The son from her second marriage to the actor survived her.

There was a short article on another inside page, together with another photograph. *Actress electrocuted in bath*, the headline announced baldly.

> Lois Delaney, formerly the toast of the West End, was discovered dead at her country home on New Year's Day. She had not been seen on the stage or on television or film for many years. Her third marriage to the property tycoon Bruce King had foundered recently and she had been living alone in seclusion while a several million pound divorce settlement was being hammered out by top London lawyers. Miss Delaney was said to have been suffering for some time from depression which had required treatment in a London clinic. An inquest is to be held.

There was a knock at the door and he knew from the crashing impact of the iron knocker that it was Naomi. She was wearing her matador's cape, moon boots and a very large fur hat that made her look like a ferocious Cossack from the Steppes.

'Found it in an old trunk up in the attic,' she said, seeing his startled expression. 'God knows where it came from. Like those coats you find hanging in the hall that must have belonged to somebody but you don't know who, or how they got there. Real fur, too. Wolf, I think, so I don't need to feel too guilty about it. Damn cold out and the snow's like ice. It must have frozen hard last night.'

She stumped into the sitting room, dislodged Thursday and sat down, rubbing her hands. The purple track suit that had appeared from beneath the cloak was made of some kind of shiny velvet. She kept the fur hat on her head.

'Now, Hugh, tell me *all*. I hear you were there when that actress woman was found dead at the Hall. It's all round the village.'

'Bad news certainly travels fast.'

'Of course it does. It's usually more interesting than good. I'd no idea Lois Delaney was living at the Hall. I remember seeing her in some play years ago and, of course, she was in that rather good television series about the rich family living in Belgrave Square. I gather she killed herself.'

'Not necessarily.'

'Well, the police will soon find out. She died in the bath, didn't she? Electrocuted. That's a horrible way to go. If I were doing it, I'd be in bed, in comfort. Lots of pills and lots of whisky and off to sleep for ever.'

'I rather agree with you.' There had been a time, at his lowest ebb after Laura had died, when he had toyed briefly with doing something exactly like that.

'Well, come on, tell me what happened.'

He told her briefly, sparing unnecessary details. 'Detective Inspector Squibb seems to be in charge of the case. You remember him from when Lady Swynford was murdered?'

'Oh, *him*.' There was deep scorn in Naomi's voice. 'He acts as though he's one of those smart-aleck TV detectives who know all the answers. I suppose there'll be an inquest.'

'I'm afraid so.'

'You'll have to go, won't you? What a bore! Did you know she was married to the very chap who bought the Hall from us – the one I was telling you about? I found that out in the newspaper.'

'I believe they were separated.'

'I don't blame her. Apparently, he buys and sells property all over the place. He also owns a chain of motels, that swanky hotel near here, and the Lord knows what else. One of the tabloid rags called him a multi-millionaire. How much do you think that means?'

'A lot of millions.'

'Well, whatever he's worth, he's a twister.'

'To be fair he hasn't made too bad a job of your old home – from what I saw of it.'

Naomi snorted. 'Did you notice the new gates?'

The colonel smiled. 'They're rather unfortunate, I agree, but the house has been pretty decently done inside. He's no cowboy. Tell me, did you ever actually meet him?'

'Only once – when he came to see the Hall. Jess and I were still living there and I showed him round. He acted as though he was going to live in it himself and, of course, I fell for it. After that, his London lawyers handled everything – beat down the price and blinded us with legal gobbledegook. Jess was already pretty ill at the time, so we weren't up to much. We must have been a walk-over.'

The colonel said, 'Lois Delaney had a son by her second marriage. He spent Christmas with her at the Hall.'

'Well, Inspector Squabb will be grilling him like a pork chop.'

'It's Squibb, Naomi. Not Squabb.'

'Who cares? Was the son there when she died?'

'No, he'd left around midday on New Year's Eve.'

'Perhaps she got depressed when he'd gone. Perhaps they'd had a row and it had upset her. If *my* son had stayed any longer at Christmas I expect we'd have been at each other's throats. Much as I love Paul, I often think it's quite a good thing that he and his family live twelve thousand miles away in Sydney.'

She stuck out her wrist and consulted the man's watch that she always wore. 'Golly, is that the time? I must go, Hugh. I promised Ruth I'd call to have a chinwag about plants.'

He saw her to the door and helped her on with the red cape. As she strode away through the snow in the direction of the Manor, the colonel was amused to observe a tell-tale glint from the front window of Miss Butler's cottage across the village green.

Freda Butler lowered the binoculars. After a while they made her arms ache and she wondered sometimes how the

U-boat captain had coped. But, of course, he would have been a strong young man and used to all the hardship and rigours of a life at sea. She had a sneaking admiration for the U-boat crews, though naturally she would never have admitted it to anybody, least of all her father, the late admiral. Of course, it was appalling how many good British seamen had been killed by the U-boats – not to mention women and evacuee children in the passenger liners – but she had read about the German losses and noted that hardly any of the U-boat crews had survived the war. There was no doubt in her mind that though they had been very wicked, they had also been very brave. Miss Butler had once suffered a panic attack on the Piccadilly Line of the London Tube and the thought of going to war sealed up in a metal tube deep under the sea was too terrifying to contemplate.

She had never been quite clear how the binoculars had come into her father's possession. She was aware – though it had never actually been discussed between them – that he had spent most of the war sailing a desk, not depth-charging enemy U-boats. At any rate, the binoculars had lain forgotten for years in a drawer and had passed to her, by chance, after his death, along with a few small chattels and a formal studio photograph of the admiral in full dress uniform. The rest of his estate had been willed to a naval museum, together with a fine oil portrait of the admiral which now hung on the museum wall and his uniform and medals which were displayed close by in a glass case. The Zeiss binoculars had not been mentioned in the will and she had not offered to hand them over as well.

Miss Butler knew that she had been a disappointment to her father. She had not been the son he had wanted, nor had she achieved high rank in the Royal Navy or had anything but a very mediocre career. Whenever she looked at his photograph she was reminded painfully of this.

After a moment, arms rested, she raised the binoculars again and made another sweep of the green. The colonel had gone back into his cottage and Naomi Grimshaw had disappeared around the corner – doubtless on her way to the Manor. Miss Butler had heard that dear Ruth was planning to open some kind of plant shop and that Mrs Grimshaw was going to help her with it. It seemed a very good idea. She didn't think they would charge the sort of high prices that the big garden centres asked and the plants would be home-grown, not raised in some foreign country and brought over in juggernaut lorries. She would like to buy a few herself for her little garden – the old-fashioned kind, not those garish modern things.

It was also rumoured that Mrs Grimshaw was going to give gardening lectures at the Manor, which would be another good thing. She had heard her speak at the Women's Institute meetings and she was always most interesting and very knowledgeable.

Now, if young Dr Harvey could persuade Ruth to marry him, they could settle down at the Manor and it would never need to be sold to outsiders or suffer the same sad fate as the Hall.

Miss Butler swept the green from side to side a few times and then stiffened, like the binoculars' original owner sighting a quarry. A car had appeared on the far side and was making its way slowly along the road, which must be exceedingly slippery after last night's hard frost. It had turned so cold that long icicles were hanging from the eaves of her cottage roof. The car didn't belong to anybody in the village – she knew them all: Dr Harvey's grey Renault; the Cuthbertsons' much-dented Escort; Mrs Grimshaw's bright red Metro; Ruth Swynford's old Land Rover; the new vicar's maroon Vauxhall, its front bumper tied on with a piece of string, and so on. This car was black and, as it stopped outside the colonel's cottage, two men got out – one young, one old. Not gentlemen – she could have told that even without the binoculars. They looked to her very much like policemen, in which case it would be to do with Miss Delaney's tragic death.

The colonel had not said anything about it when he had delivered the Save the Donkey collection. Like herself, and unlike many in the village, he was not a gossip and was always very considerate of other people's feelings. He had probably felt that the news might upset her. A most chivalrous man, as she had cause to know first-hand.

But if he *had* happened to mention Miss Delaney when he had brought the collection tin, Miss Butler might have let slip that she had known her many years ago. Not very well, it was true, but she had come across her once or twice in her Wren days when Miss Delaney had been married to one of the young naval officers – Lieutenant Roper. Miss Butler had admired the same handsome young officer herself, but of course, there had never been any question of him returning her regard.

Lois Delaney had already been a well-known name and whenever she had appeared at some cocktail party or dinner in the Mess, there had always been a great flurry of excitement, with people craning their necks and standing on tiptoe to catch a glimpse of her. Even her late father had fallen under the spell, Miss Butler recalled. He had been far nicer to Miss Delaney than he had ever been to herself and she remembered, too, how bitter she had felt about it at the time. She glanced now at the photograph of her father, prominently displayed on the top of the bureau. He stared back, his gaze tinged with impatience: the impatience that she had known so well.

She would not have told the colonel, however, that she had been aware that Miss Delaney had moved into the Hall. It had come about quite by chance. She had gone to the dentist in Dorchester some weeks ago – a tiresome toothache – and had picked up one of the daily newspapers to read in the waiting room. Not at all the sort of paper she usually read. Indeed, she had been quite shocked by its contents. Whatever was the world coming to? There had been a photograph of Miss Delaney in the gossip column, seen with her third husband who was, apparently, a very rich property tycoon. Unfortunately, the marriage had broken down and they were getting divorced. It was expected that Miss Delaney would be awarded a substantial settlement. At least ten million pounds was the figure mentioned. To Miss Butler, who subsisted on a very modest pension from the Royal Navy, such a sum was unimaginable. She had read on and discovered that, meanwhile, Miss Delaney had gone to live in one of the properties that her husband had bought and converted into flats. A large Victorian country house in a village in Dorset, near Dorchester, as it happened. Miss Butler had torn out the piece – very quietly so nobody else in the waiting room had noticed – and stowed it away in her handbag. Later, she had read it again and decided that the house in question might be none other than the Hall at Frog End.

She had toyed with the idea of calling there. She would knock at the flat door and say, 'I'm sure you don't remember me, Miss Delaney, but I'm Admiral Butler's daughter. We met many years ago.'

In her imagination, the actress replied with a warm smile, 'Of course I remember you, Miss Butler. How lovely to see you again. Do come in and have a cup of tea.'

It was some time before she had found the nerve to put this to the test and, when she did, nothing had gone as she had hoped. First of all, the Hall front door had been firmly shut and locked and the flat bells were marked by numbers without names so that she had no idea which one to ring. After a moment, she had walked round to the back of the house where there was a terrace overlooking the lawn. She could remember the gardens when the Gurney family had still been in residence and the village fête had sometimes been held there, instead of at the Manor. When Naomi Grimshaw had divorced her husband and come back to live at her former home again, she had managed to keep the beautiful gardens going with the aid of one old gardener. But then, of course, Mr and Mrs Gurney had both died and so had the gardener, and the family fortunes were clearly running out. Mrs Grimshaw and her sister had battled on but Jessica Gurney had fallen ill and, in the end, there had been little choice but to sell the Hall.

Sadly, there had been sweeping changes, Miss Butler had noted: flower beds taken out; trees and shrubs cut down and cleared to make way for new lawn; a charming Victorian gazebo removed. The old rose garden of tall and scented standards had been replanted with rows of modern dwarfs, winter-pruned to within an inch of their lives. It had all reminded her of a public municipal park, planned entirely for easy maintenance.

She had tiptoed along the terrace and peered in at a window.

A man had been sitting at a table and it had looked as though he was sewing something, though she couldn't quite see what it was. There had been a younger man, standing at his shoulder – rather a handsome young man in a foreign sort of way. She had moved on.

When she had reached the French windows she had stopped and peered in again. And that's when she had seen Lois Delaney. There was no mistaking her because although she was a lot older, she still looked much the same. The hair would have been dyed now, of course, but very expensively by some London salon so that it looked quite real, and very well cut. If you could afford to spend a lot of money on nothing but the best hairdressers and cosmetics and on exclusive designer clothes, then you had a big and rather unfair advantage, in Miss Butler's view. It was impossible, of course, on a small pension.

The actress had been talking on the telephone. Miss Butler had watched her closely for a while. She had been speaking animatedly into the mouthpiece, running her fingers through the expensively-styled and dyed hair and, every so often, picking up a glass from a table to drink from it. It looked like tomato juice but somehow Miss Butler thought there was more to it than met the eye. She knew all about innocent-looking cocktails. Her father, for instance, had favoured Horse's Necks which had passed, at a pinch, for plain ginger ale.

As she had stood by the French windows, Lois Delaney had suddenly glanced in her direction and Miss Butler had been quite certain that she had seen her. She had drawn back at once and hurried away across the terrace and down the drive, hot with shame and embarrassment. What a terrible thing she had done, trespassing on private property and looking in people's windows! There had been no question of her returning and no question of mentioning the incident to the colonel; or to anybody else.

The younger of the two men was knocking at the door of Pond Cottage and Miss Butler adjusted the binoculars to see him more clearly. He looked very much like that unpleasant inspector who had been in charge of the investigation into Lady Swynford's death and who had gone round upsetting everybody with his questions – herself included. Thank goodness she'd kept quiet about her little visit to the Hall. There was no reason for him to bother her this time. Miss Butler's heart suddenly skipped a beat and her hand went to her throat. Unless, of course, somebody else had seen her.

Six

Detective Inspector Squibb wiped his feet on the mat and advanced into the hallway of Pond Cottage, his sergeant close behind.

'Just a few more questions, if you don't mind, sir.' His manner made it clear that if the colonel did mind, it was too bad.

He showed them into the sitting room and invited them to sit down. The inspector appropriated the wing chair by the fire while the sergeant, to Thursday's disgust, parked himself heavily at the other end of the sofa, disturbing the cushions and the cat in the process.

'How can I help you, Inspector?'

'You said in your statement, sir, that you told Mrs Barnes to stay in the bedroom while you went into the bathroom?'

'That's right. It could have distressed her unnecessarily and there was also the danger of electric shock.'

'Did you go back into the bedroom when you had discovered Miss Delaney?'

'No. I called out to Mrs Barnes to phone the police. Then I stayed with the body until they came.'

'So, in fact, Mrs Barnes was out of your sight. She could have touched or moved things without your knowing?'

'I suppose so.'

'She says she didn't.'

'Then I would believe her, Inspector. She seems a very trustworthy person.'

'People do the strangest things, sir – often when they're trying to protect someone. I'm not convinced that Mrs

Barnes has told us everything. There was no suicide note found, you know.'

'Perhaps Miss Delaney didn't bother to write one.'

'Suicides usually do. It's all part of the drama they're creating, and they often don't want other people to get the blame.'

The colonel recalled the young recruit in his company who had hanged himself and the gunner who had blown his brains out. Neither had left any kind of note. 'In my army experience, that's not always the case.'

The inspector went down another track. 'But we did find a large number of empty vodka bottles. Did you know that Miss Delaney drank?'

'I didn't know anything about her private life, Inspector.'

'Mrs Barnes admitted that she used to clear out the empties every so often. She said Miss Delaney used telephone orders from an off-licence in Dorchester and they would deliver them.'

'A lot of people do that. Myself included. It saves carting heavy bottles around.'

'Her husband, Mr King, told us that she'd been drinking since before she met him. Apparently, she'd started when her career nose-dived and she wasn't getting any more parts. She'd been in and out of one of those expensive drying-out clinics in London and when they got married she gave up the booze for several years, but then she went back on it again. He said she'd also been treated for depression and six months ago she tried to kill herself, swallowing a lot of pills with the drink. Luckily he found her in time.'

'When did they separate, as a matter of interest?'

'Three months ago. He suggested she take one of the flats at the Hall for the time being while the divorce was going through – until she'd decided where she wanted to live. He said she was getting a pretty generous settlement. She'd have no money worries.'

'Mrs Barnes told me that Mr King came to see his wife at the Hall on New Year's Eve. I wonder why?'

'She'd asked him to. Wrote a letter to him just before

Christmas, he said, and, as he happened to be going to inspect some property in the area, he decided to call by on his way back to London. He thought it would be some argument over the divorce – but instead she told him she'd been offered a leading part in a revival of a play. A West End theatre had apparently come up with an available slot and all that was needed was for someone to put up the cash. She asked him if he'd do it. Begged him – he said. Told him it would save her life – those were her very words to him.'

'And did he agree?'

'No, he refused point-blank. It was some old play that hadn't been put on in London for years. Something called *Hay Wire* or *Hay Wagon*, I think he said.'

'*Hay Fever*. It's by Noël Coward.'

'Before my time, I'm afraid, sir. Anyway, Mr King was sure it would flop and, in any case, he didn't think his wife was up to it – physically, or mentally. She made a big scene, he said. Drunk and crying and yelling at him, but he stuck to his guns. Now, of course, he blames himself partly for what happened.'

'You mean that she killed herself? But I don't believe she did.'

'Why is that, sir?'

He shrugged. 'Just a hunch.'

The inspector smiled faintly. 'I'm afraid the police need rather more than hunches, sir. We need evidence and, so far, all the evidence points to suicide. Miss Delaney's state of mind, the disappointment over losing her one chance of making a big comeback, the fact that she was drunk, which would have affected any normal, rational judgement.'

He nodded. 'Yes, it does seem to add up. But it's a complicated way to have done it. An overdose of pills would have been so much easier and pleasanter.'

'There's always the risk of being found and revived, sir – same as happened before. It was quite easy, if you think about it. All she had to do was run the bath, plug the hairdryer into the electric power point outside the bathroom door, switch on, take it into the bathroom, get into the bath, start the dryer and put it in the water. Bingo!'

'Why take all her clothes off? Would any woman want to be found like that? Particularly an older woman?'

'She was an actress, sir. You know what they're like. Show-offs. Proper drama queens. Like that woman floating along in that poem.'

'The Lady of Shalott?'

'That's the one. They made us learn it at school and it went on for ever. I could still recite it. *On either side the river lie . . .*'

'I'll take your word for it,' the colonel said hastily. 'It still seems odd though. Perhaps someone else got into the flat? An intruder? A deranged fan?'

'It would have to have been somebody she knew to gain admittance. There's a security system on the outer door and a peep hole in the flat door.'

'Mrs Barnes said that Miss Delaney's husband reported that the flat's outside bell was faulty; he couldn't make it work and had to use the caretaker's bell.'

'We checked the system but there doesn't seem to be a anything wrong with it. Miss Delaney probably wasn't answering, or didn't hear it. In any case, it's unthinkable that she would have admitted a complete stranger. Mrs Barnes said she was very jumpy about her security. That was one reason why she'd gone to live at the Hall. She felt safe there.'

'What about somebody getting in through a window?'

'The windows have very good security locks, sir, including the French windows leading on to the terrace. They were all closed and locked with no sign of tampering, bolts in place – and you can only do them from the inside. Also, there were no tracks in the snow outside. Not a single footprint.' Another smile. 'We do know our job, sir.'

'I'm sure you do, Inspector. But it snowed heavily for most of the night. Any tracks made earlier would have been obliterated.'

'Like I said, sir, the fact is that nobody forced any of the windows or the doors. Nobody got in that way; or out either.'

'Where were the keys?'

'Where they were always kept – on a hook fitted beside the French windows for the purpose. Mrs Barnes showed us. They were all there.'

'What about fingerprints?'

'I can tell you read detective stories, sir! The only finger-prints on the windows or doors belonged to Miss Delaney and to Mrs Barnes, who did the cleaning.'

'And in the rest of the flat?'

'Just ones that had good reason to be there: Miss Delaney's; Mr and Mrs Barnes's; Miss Hayes'; Mr King's and ones that belong to Mr Farrell, Miss Delaney's son.' Inspector Squibb paused. 'We had some trouble tracking him down.'

'Oh?'

'He'd gone to a New Year's Eve celebration in Scotland . . . some castle in the middle of nowhere. The party went on for a long time.'

The colonel said drily, 'The Scots take their New Year's Eves very seriously.'

'So I've heard. Mr Farrell spent Christmas with his mother, you know.'

'Yes, Mrs Barnes mentioned that.'

'You seem to have had quite a conversation with Mrs Barnes, sir.'

'We have something in common, Inspector. We made the unfortunate discovery of Miss Delaney's body together.'

'Did she happen to speak of a Miss Quinn who lives on the first floor?'

'No. But I think I met her when I was collecting for the donkey fund.'

'I'll bet she didn't give a penny to it.'

'People aren't obliged to, Inspector.'

'No, but I know the type, sir. Mean as anything. She seems to spend her time snooping. Told me she'd seen Mr King arrive and leave. And that she'd noticed one of the residents ringing the bell of Miss Delaney's flat on New Year's Eve.'

'Really?'

'A Miss Jeanette Hayes. She lives on the top floor. Paints china plates for a living.'

'Yes, I met her when I was collecting.'

'Miss Hayes admitted to us that she went down around half past seven, to ask Miss Delaney if she'd like to have a New Year's Eve drink with her. She thought she might be feeling lonely. But when there was no answer she gave up. I asked her why she didn't just give her a ring – save her going all the way downstairs – but she didn't have the number. It's ex-directory.'

'Did she know Miss Delaney?'

'Oh, yes. She'd been living with her son, Rex Farrell, for several years till they split up. She knew her very well.'

'That's quite a coincidence.'

'Yes, isn't it, sir? I thought so. In fact, she wasn't the only resident who was acquainted with Miss Delaney. Mr Neville Avery told us he knew her. It seems he designed stage costumes for her some years ago.'

'Is that so?'

'He makes dolls now. Dolls for grown-ups. People collect them, he said. It takes all sorts to make a world, doesn't it, sir?'

The colonel ignored the smirk. 'Yes, it does, Inspector. Otherwise it would be a very dull place.'

'Very true, sir. And by the way, our snooper, Miss Quinn, mentioned spotting something else, too. Not on New Year's Eve, though. About two weeks ago she said she happened to be glancing out of her window one morning and she caught sight of a woman creeping along the terrace and looking in through the windows. She told us that the woman spent a long time outside Miss Delaney's flat, spying on her.'

'Another resident?'

'No, she didn't recognize her at all. Thought she must have been somebody from the village. She said she was elderly and dressed in navy blue – navy coat, navy lace-up shoes, navy felt hat. She noticed that there was some kind of gilt brooch on her coat lapel – the sort of thing someone connected with one of the Armed Services might wear. Does that description ring any bells with you, sir?'

It did. But he shook his head. 'I'm afraid not, Inspector.'

'Probably some old biddy trying to get a glimpse of her idol. Some obsessive fans will travel for miles and wait for hours. You'd be amazed.'

What *was* amazing him at that moment was that Thursday was graciously allowing Sergeant Biddlecombe to tickle him under the chin. And not only allowing it but positively encouraging him – stretching his neck out, eyes shut in bliss. The picture of amiable docility.

'Nice cat, sir,' the sergeant said. 'I've two of my own.'

He could have told the sergeant that Thursday was anything but nice but he refrained, just as he had refrained from identifying the mysterious woman dressed all in navy blue with the service gilt brooch.

'Well, if that's all, Inspector . . .'

'For the moment, sir. Our inquiries are ongoing.'

'What does that mean exactly?'

'That we're exploring all possibilities.'

When the two policemen had gone, he threw another log on the fire, reclaimed his wing chair, unpleasantly warm from Inspector Squibb's backside, and sat thinking for a while, hands resting on the padded arms. Inspector Squibb hadn't mentioned that Roy Ward had also been acquainted with Lois Delaney, which was rather odd. Unless he hadn't known about it because Roy Ward hadn't told him.

He thought of another odd thing: if Lois Delaney had been intent on committing suicide, why on earth would she bother about putting pine essence in the bath water? Relaxation could hardly have been the uppermost thing on her mind. The inspector would no doubt have explained it as setting the dramatic scene.

Thursday turned around twice to resettle himself on the

sofa, rested his chin on his front paws and blinked his yellow eyes.

'You're a wicked old fraudster,' the colonel remarked to the cat. 'And so am I. Neither of us is to be trusted an inch.'

Miss Butler had the colonel under close observation as he walked across the village green – though without the aid of the binoculars, this time. She had just happened to be doing a little dusting in the sitting room when she had caught sight of him coming out of his cottage. She watched him approaching, wondering where he was going, and was very, very surprised when he made directly for her gate and opened it. Good gracious, whatever could he want? The Save the Donkey collection had been safely delivered and counted, the leftover badges returned. The summer fête was months away, the churchyard grass would not need cutting till early spring and, in any case, the grass rota was not her concern: Mr Townsend was in charge of that. There was the coming jumble sale, of course, where she was manning a stall. Perhaps he wanted to contribute some old clothes? Or maybe he was going to volunteer to help with another collection, which would be very good news, what with Major Cuthbertson being so unreliable. She had spotted the major going into the Dog and Duck and had her doubts that he had ever really been ill at all.

The colonel gave a quiet knock at the door and Miss Butler stuffed the duster hurriedly into a drawer and went to answer it, feeling rather flustered. After all, she was not accustomed to receiving gentlemen at the cottage – except the vicar. The sitting room was very small, for one thing, and for another she felt it to be somewhat improper. Not that anybody took much notice of that sort of thing these days, of course, and the dear colonel was above suspicion.

'Do come in, Colonel. I'm afraid you've caught me unawares. Everything in a bit of a mess.'

She went ahead of him into the neat little sitting room and straightened cushions and the cloth on the side table, none of which needed straightening at all. He seemed to take up a lot of room and he could scarcely stand upright because of the low ceiling. Fortunately, the new vicar was a much smaller man.

'Do mind your head on the beams, won't you? Would you like some tea?' She was wondering anxiously if he would mind the cheap kind she always bought. Perhaps he usually drank Earl Grey? Or some kind of Chinese tea, since he had spent many years abroad?

But, no, he didn't want any tea, so they sat down and he smiled at her in a reassuring sort of way.

'I'm very sorry to intrude like this, Miss Butler.'

'Oh, not at all, Colonel. Not at all.' What on earth could he want? She fussed a little with her navy cardigan, pulling the sleeves further down at her wrists.

'I'll come straight to the point,' he said. 'If you don't mind. It's about Lois Delaney.'

Her mouth fell open. 'Miss Delaney? Whatever do you mean?'

'I wondered if you knew her at all?'

Miss Butler froze, warning bells ringing. She said carefully, 'Only very slightly. I came across her when I was serving in the Wrens. She was married to a naval officer. Her first husband, I believe.'

'Did you happen to go to see her when she moved into the Hall?

She stared at the colonel. 'I . . . I . . .'

'Because when the police came to see me about her death, they mentioned that someone had been seen on the terrace about two weeks earlier – looking in at Miss Delaney's flat window. A lady. They had a very good description of her.'

'Did they?' Her voice sounded like a mouse's squeak.

'Dressed all in navy blue and wearing some kind of gilt service brooch. Naturally, they're investigating all possible leads.'

'Yes, naturally.'

'But so far they haven't discovered who this particular person was. They asked me if the description matched anybody that I knew in the village.'

She gulped. 'And what did you say, Colonel?'

'I told them that it didn't. You have nothing to fear from me, Miss Butler, but I would just like your assurance that there is no connection whatsoever between the unknown lady on the terrace and the death of Miss Delaney. And I'm perfectly sure that there isn't.' He smiled at her gently. 'We're already fellow conspirators, aren't we? We trust each other completely.'

He was alluding, of course, to her theft of Lady Swynford's diamond brooch at the summer garden fête and the fact that he had not given her away to the police. She had already returned the brooch, in fact, but he had kept her shameful secret, saved her from disgrace, and the matter had never been mentioned between them again. She still did not know what had come over her to have done such a wicked thing.

'Yes, indeed, Colonel.'

'So perhaps you could just put my mind at rest?'

She told him the whole story, from the brief encounters with Miss Delaney at the naval receptions, to the accidental discovery in the tabloid newspaper that she had moved into the Hall and her failed attempt to call.

'I meant no harm, Colonel. Please believe me. I was just curious. Such a fascinating woman, you know. My father was greatly taken by her.'

They both looked up at the bemedalled studio portrait of the admiral on top of the bureau glowering down.

'Yes, most people seem to have been.'

She gabbled on. 'I looked through the window and saw Miss Delaney. She was on the telephone, talking to someone. Looking very pleased about something, actually. Very happy. Then she turned my way and I think she caught sight of me. Of course, I left immediately.' Freda Butler put her hand over her eyes, mortified. 'I never went back, please believe me, or tried to see her again and I'm very ashamed of what I did.'

The colonel reached out and touched her arm. 'Of course I believe you, Miss Butler. And there's no more to be said.'

'You won't tell the police?'

'Certainly not. It has no bearing on the case. We'll keep it between ourselves, shall we?'

He stood up and she saw him to the front door.

She said, 'Thank you, Colonel. Thank you so much.'

'There's nothing to thank me for, Miss Butler, and nothing to worry about.'

He looked up at the sky and said briskly, as though everything was perfectly normal, 'Do you know, I do believe it might be going to snow again.'

Seven

At the inquest on the death of Lois Delaney, the public gallery of the Coroner's Court was crowded and the national newspapers had sent their reporters. She might have been a faded star, but Lois Delaney was still managing to pull in an audience.

Witnesses were called, one after the other, to the box below the bench and sworn in. Inspector Squibb described the discovery of the body and the scene; no marks or trace of a break-in anywhere from outside the house or at the main entrance and none at the flat windows, or the flat door in the hall. The police doctor testified that Lois Delaney had died somewhere between six and eight o'clock in the evening in question – the warm bath water had made a precise assessment difficult. There had been no signs of a struggle. Death had been due to electric shock caused by a hairdryer connected to a power socket outside the bathroom being immersed in the bath while switched on. The pathologist who had performed a post-mortem on the body added the information that Lois Delaney had drunk considerably more than half a bottle of vodka mixed with tomato juice. Her liver had shown signs of permanent damage but the other organs were healthy. The coroner was busy making notes with his fountain pen.

Dr Harvey was called about the occasion a week previously when Miss Delaney had summoned him to her flat at the Hall.

'She had run out of the nitrazepam sleeping pills normally provided by her London doctor and asked me to prescribe more.'

The coroner asked, 'And did you, Doctor?'

'No, I prescribed a placebo for her instead.'

'Why was that?'

'It's often just as effective as the real thing, and it's a lot safer. When I saw her, Miss Delaney had obviously been drinking. Sleeping pills and alcohol are a dangerous combination, and she was living alone. I wasn't prepared to take the risk.'

'How did Miss Delaney seem to you, Dr Harvey? What was her emotional state at that time?"

'I thought she seemed rather distressed.'

'Did she tell you why?'

'She said she hated it when she couldn't sleep.'

'Did she strike you as being unbalanced?'

'I'm not qualified to say.'

A London psychiatrist who had treated Lois Delaney during her stays in a drying-out clinic gave evidence that in addition to her dependence on alcohol, she had suffered from severe depression. He had prescribed medication with some degree of success but the condition was always likely to return and had done so repeatedly in Miss Delaney's case over several years. Yes, she could be described as having an unbalanced temperament . . . that is to say, subject to extreme mood swings and inclined to irrational behaviour and judgement. And she had told him that she frequently felt an urge to take her own life. In his professional opinion, this was what she had ultimately done.

The London doctor who had prescribed the nitrazepam was also called and testified that the actress often had great difficulty sleeping and had become psychologically dependent on the drug, which had a diminishing effect with time. She had attempted suicide six months ago by taking an overdose of the pills on top of alcohol, but fortunately her husband had discovered her in time. As her doctor, he had been reducing the dose gradually in an effort to wean her off the drug but in cases like Miss Delaney's, where the patient was not anxious to co-operate, it always took time.

Mrs Barnes was called and, plainly very nervous, confirmed that Miss Delaney had often seemed depressed, and that she was aware that she drank more than was good for her.

The coroner wrote some more notes. 'Do you know how much?'

'I couldn't say exactly, sir, but there were always a lot of empty bottles.'

A faint titter sounded around the courtroom. The coroner glanced up, frowning.

'What effect would you say that drinking too much had on her?'

'It made her feel very down, sir. She'd cry a lot and say how much she missed the theatre.'

'Did she ever speak of taking her own life?'

'No, sir. Not to me, or to my husband either. She never said anything about that, but we were always worried that she might harm herself when she was in one of those moods.'

The hairdryer had been a brand new one, Mrs Barnes testified. The old one had broken down and Miss Delaney had asked her to get another for her. She had gone to Boots in Dorchester and bought one – a white one because Miss Delaney liked light colours. It had a metal stand and was kept out on the dressing table in the bedroom, same as the old one had been. Miss Delaney went to her hairdresser's in London regularly and had it cut very nicely, but in between she washed her hair herself with the hand shower in the bathroom and she always sat at her dressing table to dry it so she could see in the mirror. She had beautiful hair, Mrs Barnes added – it was quite easy to look after.

'So far as you are aware, she never used the electric socket outside the bathroom door so that she could dry her hair inside the bathroom?'

'No, never, sir. The mirror's over the basin and right on the other side of the bathroom. The cord wouldn't have reached far enough for her to see properly. Besides, Miss Delaney was frightened of electricity and she always got my husband to change light bulbs, for instance. And she knew how dangerous it could be near water. She told me a friend of hers had been electrocuted that way. I know she'd never have done a silly thing like that – except on purpose.'

'Do you know if it was her custom to take a bath early in the evenings?'

'Yes, sir. She told me that she'd always done that when she wasn't working in the theatre. She said she liked to have a bath around six o'clock, then spend the rest of the evening in her dressing gown. She found it more comfortable and she didn't have the bother of undressing twice. It also made her sleep better. She didn't always sleep very well, like the doctor said.'

At this point, Mrs Barnes's voice faltered and she groped for a handkerchief.

The coroner said gently, 'This must be very upsetting for you, Mrs Barnes. Would you like to take a rest for a while?'

She rallied bravely, wiping her eyes. 'No, thank you, sir. I'm all right.'

'Mr King was her only visitor that evening?'

'As far as I know, sir.'

'What time did he arrive at the Hall?'

'It would have been about quarter past five. I let him in myself because he hadn't been able to make the outside bell to Miss Delaney's flat work.'

'He didn't have a key to the main door?'

'Yes, he did, sir, but he didn't have it with him. The visit was on the spur of the moment, he said. Miss Delaney had asked him to call by and he happened to be in the area.'

'Do you know what time he left the Hall?'

'Just past six. He came to tell my husband to be sure and get the bell mended.'

'Did you see him out?'

'Oh, yes, sir. My husband and I both went to the door with him and waited till he'd driven away.'

Jeanette Hayes was summoned. Her long hair was tied back and she was wearing a navy reefer jacket over her jeans. She looked pale, the colonel thought, and tense. She testified that she had rung at the door of Flat 2 that evening at about half past seven and had received no answer.

'You were acquainted with Miss Delaney?'

'Yes. I'd known her through her son, Rex. I lived with him for several years but we broke up last summer. That was when I moved to the Hall.'

'Were you aware that Miss Delaney was a resident?'

'She wasn't – not at that time. When she moved in, it was a complete surprise to me.'

'You weren't aware that it was her husband who had bought and converted the Hall into flats?'

'No. I dealt with a company called Greenhill Estates. I didn't know it had anything to do with Mr King.'

'Did you visit Miss Delaney after she'd moved in?'

'I didn't realize she had for some weeks – not until I happened to meet her in the hall.'

'Did you see much of Miss Delaney after that meeting?'

'I didn't see her again at all until Rex came to stay with her at Christmas. She invited me for a drink on Christmas Eve.'

'And you accepted?'

'Yes. She didn't tell me that Rex was there, or I wouldn't have done.'

'Why not?'

'I wasn't anxious to see him again. Our relationship was finished.'

'How did you find Miss Delaney on that particular evening? What sort of mood was she in?'

'She was in very high spirits. She'd been offered a leading part in a Noël Coward revival and she was certain it would be a big success.'

The colonel was called next. He answered the same questions all over again. He had found Miss Delaney dead in the bath; he had neither touched nor moved anything, nor seen any kind of note that she might have left. And, no, he had never met her before or knew anything of her private life. As he reached the end of his testimony, he was tempted to offer his own personal conviction – that whatever the evidence pointed to, Lois Delaney had not killed herself. But on what could he base it? That her mouth was half-open and that she had looked as though she had wanted to speak to him? The coroner would think he was as unbalanced as the dead woman. And, in any case, witnesses at an inquest were there to answer questions, not offer uninvited opinions.

The next witness was Lois Delaney's son, Rex Farrell, and the colonel could see a strong resemblance to his mother. Somewhere in his mid-thirties, dark-haired, good-looking, a rich speaking voice and a great deal of easy charm. He was an actor, he said. He lived in Fulham in London and he had spent Christmas with his mother in her flat at the Hall. She had been on unusually good form because of the chance of returning to the stage in the Noël Coward play. Over the moon, in fact.

'Would you describe your late mother as subject to mood swings?'

'Lord, yes. It depended how things were going for her.'

'What things, precisely?'

'In the theatre. It was the only thing she really cared about.'

The son said it without rancour, the colonel noted. It was probably something that he had accepted at a very early age.

'Were you aware that she had tried to take her life six months ago?'

'I found out about it later. She told me so herself. Actually, she said she hadn't really meant to do it; she'd drunk too much and forgotten how many pills she'd taken.'

'You didn't hear about it first from her husband – your stepfather?'

Rex Farrell smiled faintly. 'We don't communicate.'

'When did you end your Christmas visit to your mother?'

'I left on the morning of the thirty-first – just before midday, as far as I can remember. I'd had an invitation to a New Year's Eve party at friends in Scotland.'

'You drove straight there?'

'I wouldn't say straight, exactly. It started to snow on the way up which made things pretty difficult. In fact, I didn't get there until early the following morning. I'd got stuck in a drift and had to spend most of that night in the car before someone came along and helped dig me out.'

There were several more questions before the coroner said, 'One final question, Mr Farrell. 'When you left your mother on the thirty-first of December, how would you describe her mood then – at that exact moment when you said goodbye?'

'Very good. She was still talking about the play and how wonderful it was going to be, being back on the stage.'

'So you had no reason to think that she had any intention of ending her life?'

'None whatsoever.'

The son had obviously not been anything like as successful as the mother. His name meant nothing to the colonel and he couldn't recall ever seeing him on the stage, on television or in any film, or mentioned in the newspapers. He must belong to the legions of unknowns who scrape a living playing bit parts in soaps and series – such as Mrs Barnes had mentioned. He wondered what the coroner thought of him and his testimony – delivered so glibly. Rex Farrell was not a witness to inspire confidence or the belief that he was necessarily telling the truth.

He watched with interest as Lois Delaney's husband took the stand. He was a thick-set man of medium height, grey-haired and dressed in what were probably very expensive clothes but not ostentatiously so. He wore none of the knuckle-duster rings or flashy gold watches that the colonel might have expected from Naomi's twister. He identified himself as head of the BHK Group of companies and testified that he had been married to Lois Delaney for nine and a half years. His evidence, delivered in a northern accent, was straightforward and unhesitating. His wife had written to him before Christmas, asking him to come and see her. He'd been reluctant to do so, thinking it was probably to do with the divorce proceedings which, in his view, were best left entirely to their lawyers. In the event, he had happened to be in the vicinity of Frog End on the 31st of December, inspecting a property, and had decided to call in at the Hall on his way back to London. Normally, he would have been using his helicopter for the trip but the weather forecast had been very bad, so he'd taken his car instead. He had arrived at the Hall at around quarter past five.

'I thought I'd have a drink with her, for old time's sake. Wish her a Happy New Year.'

The coroner said, 'Was there any animosity between you and your wife, on account of the divorce proceedings?'

'None at all. We'd both agreed that the marriage had ended and the divorce was being worked out perfectly amicably.'

When are divorces ever thus? the colonel wondered.

'What did your wife want to see you about?'

'It was nothing to do with the divorce. She wanted me to put up the money for a play she'd been asked to appear in. A revival of an old Noël Coward one, she told me. She was very keen on the idea but she said that she didn't trust the people who were supposed to be putting up the money not to pull out. It had happened once before in her career and she was terrified of that happening again. Especially this time.'

'What was your response?'

'I refused. I'd put up money for another play soon after we were married and lost the lot.'

'How did she react to your refusal?'

'She became hysterical. Made a big scene. She'd been drinking before I arrived – I could tell that – and she went completely out of control. She said it would save her life if she could get back into the theatre – it wasn't worth living otherwise. She kept begging me for the money and I kept refusing. She'd obviously convinced herself that the backers would let her down – that nobody had confidence in her any more. I told her that she could use her own money, once the divorce was through – if that's what she really wanted. She was being given a very generous settlement. Twenty million pounds.'

There was an audible intake of breath in the courtroom.

'And what did she say to that?'

'She said it would be too late. The money was needed immediately or the chance could be gone. She couldn't bear it if that happened. I felt very sorry for her, but I'm a businessman and I thought the play was too old-fashioned and bound to flop. In any case, she wasn't up to acting on stage – not with her depression and her addiction to alcohol. I'd lived with her for nearly ten years and I'd seen at first-hand what she was like. She was beyond reason, though. In the end, I'm afraid I just walked out and left her.'

'What time was that?'

'I'm not sure – around six o'clock, I'd say. I hadn't stayed long, in the circumstances.'

'Did it occur to you that she might try to take her own life – as she had done once before?'

'No, I'm afraid it didn't. She often made dramatic scenes and, to be honest, I was fed up with them. With hindsight, I see I should have played things along and I regret it very much now. Our marriage had failed but I still admired my wife; she was a very beautiful and extraordinarily talented woman.'

'You heard your wife's son, Mr Farrell, testify that his mother seemed in very good spirits when he left her at midday on New Year's Eve – as she had been while he was staying with her over Christmas. Do you have any comment to make on that?'

'Yes, I have. My wife had been alone for more than five hours by the time I arrived. It was plenty of time for her to change moods, not to mention drink a good deal. Mr Farrell knows that as well as I do. And he knows exactly what his mother was like.' Bruce King didn't trouble to conceal contempt for his stepson. 'He's well aware that she'd been treated for severe depression for years and that she had a big problem with alcohol. And my wife was also an actress. She was very good at concealing her feelings if she chose to. Mr Farrell knew that, too.'

The colonel drove home slowly through the snow. The road surface was treacherously slippery, especially on the back lanes, and the old Riley he'd had since the Fifties kept slithering and sliding. It was temperamental at the best of times and he supposed that he really ought to trade it in for some new and modern car. One that started first go, that had a heater that worked, electric windows, convenient central locking, that ran for miles on diesel and had spare parts that were easy to order. But he didn't want to. The Riley had character. It had a soul. It was quite unlike all the identical runabouts with meaningless names, easy-to-pronounce in any language. Besides, he had driven the Riley with Laura sitting at his side and she had loved it too.

By the time he reached the village green, it was dark, the lights from the other houses twinkling away across the snow. Miss Butler's sitting room curtains were drawn, he noticed, so she would be off-watch, so to speak. Poor Miss Butler! He had believed her poignant little story completely, as he had believed her before about the diamond brooch. Living her humdrum life, she had made a brave bid to consort with glamour and fame only for it to end in ignominy. There had seemed no need whatever to breathe a word to Inspector Squibb, and there was even less need now.

The coroner had been satisfied that Lois Delaney had taken her own life. She had committed suicide while the balance of her mind had been disturbed. Condolences had been expressed to the family. The case was closed.

Thursday was fast asleep on the sofa but he came into the kitchen and wound himself round the colonel's legs. It was time for supper and he was prepared to show some affection to get it. The colonel opened a tin of best quality tuna chunks and mashed them up in the china pet dish which bore the word *DOG* on the side. Since Thursday couldn't read, this hadn't seemed to matter when he'd bought it. The old cat approached the dish with caution and sniffed at the contents.

'If you don't like it, it's too bad,' the colonel told him firmly, not prepared to indulge in cat fads. 'That's all you're getting.'

He went into the sitting room and with the aid of a fire-lighter and some kindling, the logs in the inglenook were soon blazing away. He poured a whisky, put one of his

Gilbert and Sullivan records on the player and sat down in the wing chair to listen. The tunes generally lifted him out of a low mood.

> *Take a pair of sparkling eyes,*
> *Hidden, ever and anon,*
> *In a merciful eclipse –*
> *Do not heed their mild surprise –*
> *Having passed the Rubicon,*
> *Take a pair of rosy lips . . .*

But he found himself thinking of Lois Delaney – of the beautiful green eyes wide open in surprise and now unmercifully eclipsed, and the red lips that had been silenced for ever.

Eight

'Hellebores,' Naomi Grimshaw said. 'Beautiful things and coming into flower now so they're just the thing to cheer you up, Hugh. You've been looking a bit down in the mouth lately and we can't have that.'

She was wearing her fuzzy white tracksuit – the one that made her look rather like an escaped polar bear – surmounted by the wolf-fur hat. A strange animal mix.

'You could plant them in that bed by the wall near the back door. They like some shade, so it'd suit them down to the ground. My favourite's *Helleborus argutifolius* – evergreen leaves and sort of lime green flowers. But Ruth's got other kinds she could let you have.'

She had plonked herself on the sofa where, for once, Thursday had vacated his seat and gone off somewhere in the garden. The colonel listened politely while his neighbour delivered a stern mini-lecture.

'That herbaceous border of yours is still a mess, Hugh. We must make a proper plan of action. The trick is to divide it up into blocks, leaving spaces for the birds to fly through. Have you got a piece of paper and pencil handy?'

He fetched both and sat obediently beside her as she sketched with quick, blunt strokes.

'You want to get some plants that'll keep flowering all through the summer – otherwise, if you're not careful you'll be left with nothing but green when the earlier ones have finished. Green's a lovely colour, of course, but you want other colours as well and you need to work out where you need them most. For instance, you could plant asters here and double cranesbills there, and scabious over here and the bronze-coloured euphorbia. They're all long-flowering.

And how about good old cat mint along the front? Thursday would like that – not that one's asking him – and it starts flowering in May and goes on all summer, particularly if you give it a haircut in June. White's a wonderful colour too, don't forget – specially against dark leaves.' She went on, filling in the blocks and suggesting more things. 'I'd go for some *Erysimum* – that does purple flowers from spring to late autumn, and *Astrantia major* Roma would look good in the middle here.'

It was interesting, he thought, that, unlike other words, Naomi seemed to get the spelling of plants exactly right – or as far as he could tell. The pencil paused.

'And, by the way, Hugh, you ought to do something about making a terrace at the back of the cottage.'

'A terrace? Do I really need one?' he said doubtfully.

'Yes, you do. Somewhere nice to sit out and look at the garden. Not one of those fake stone horrors, of course. Real old flags. You can find them in that reclamation place outside Dorchester. They'll cost a bit, but it would be worth it and Ruth's gardener chap, Jacob, will lay them properly for you and not charge you a fortune. Pay him cash, of course. You get the sun coming round there for most of the day until it goes down. Just the place to sit with a drink on a nice warm evening and watch the sun go down.'

It suddenly occurred to the colonel that Naomi was probably thinking more about her sundowners than his personal summer enjoyment. He smiled inwardly.

'I'll certainly give it consideration.'

'It's a jolly good idea of mine.' Naomi rose to her feet. 'Well, I must be off. The dogs need a walk.' Her two Jack Russells, Mutt and Jeff, occasionally came with her into his garden where they kept a respectful distance from Thursday's claws. At the cottage front door, she paused. 'I meant to ask you about the inquest. How did it go?'

'The verdict was suicide.'

'Yes, I read that in the newspaper. Do you believe it?'

He said cautiously, 'The evidence pointed to it.'

'Huh! If I was going to be handed twenty million pounds

on a plate, like she was, the last thing I'd be planning would be suicide.'

He watched her stride away down the snowy path. Suicide would indeed be the last thing Naomi would *ever* contemplate – with or without the twenty million – he thought wryly. His neighbour was too well-equipped to withstand the buffetings of life; a sturdy oak compared with the frail reed that had been Lois Delaney.

He sat down for a moment and thought about what Naomi had said – not about the planting plan, although that had sounded inspiring, or about the sundowner terrace – but about the twenty million pounds. It was certainly a very large sum indeed but he was not so sure that Lois Delaney cared all that much about money. Her son had stated in court that the only thing his mother had really cared about had been the theatre. And he should know.

Nine

The funeral of Lois Delaney took place the following week. Arrangements had been made for her to be buried in the churchyard at Frog End and it was rumoured in the village that her tycoon husband had made a substantial contribution to the church fabric fund in order for the grave to be sited prominently near the front instead of stuck out of sight round the back. Several coaches had been laid on for mourners to travel from London and the twelfth-century church which normally had a congregation of around seventy – Christmas and Easter excepted – was full to overflowing. The pathway leading up to the west door was lined with expensive bouquets and wreaths and, inside, the altar and the aisles had been decorated with masses of pure white flowers. The pale oak coffin – lying in its solitary state in the chancel – was adorned with an enormous cross of lilies.

The colonel had found a seat at the end of a side pew, next to a blonde dressed in cherry red. Few people wore black clothes to funerals these days – not even black ties – which seemed a pity, he thought. The dead deserved some outward show of respect. He didn't know the blonde's name but her face was vaguely familiar. So were other faces in the congregation and several of them were famous.

Inserted at the end of a stiff service sheet was an open invitation to refreshments afterwards at the Chilcote Hotel. The colonel had never been there but he had heard that it was the ultimate in country house luxury. An eighteen-hole golf course; floodlit tennis courts; indoor and outdoor heated swimming pools; jacuzzis; whirlpool baths in every suite;

saunas and massage parlours; fitness gymnasium . . . everything the stressed and jaded and very rich could want or
need. Naomi had, predictably, deemed it the last word in
vulgarity. Like the Hall, it had once been a private house,
but far larger and grander – a very stately home to one
family for several hundred years who had eventually fallen
on hard times. Apparently, Bruce King had snapped it up
when they had fallen to their lowest ebb and turned it into
the luxury hotel.

The new young vicar, Naomi's happy-clappy type,
seemed overawed by the size and importance of the
congregation, as well as by the occasion, and kept stum-
bling over his words. Fortunately, he had left his guitar
behind and the village organist, Miss Hartshorne, had
been ousted by a pale and long-haired stranger from
London who coaxed a miraculous sound from the wheezy
old instrument.

They sang beautiful hymns: *Dear Lord and Father of
Mankind, The King of Love My Shepherd Is* and *Abide With
Me*. A very famous actor gave a moving eulogy, praising
Lois Delaney's great beauty and talent and the pleasure she
had given to generations of theatregoers. A radiant light
had gone out, he said, with just the right touch of suppressed
emotion in his voice, and it could never be rekindled.

The colonel completely agreed with him.

The coffin was borne out into the snowy churchyard
and the mourners gathered around the open grave – extras
to the final starring role of Lois Delaney. The colonel
stood at a distance, listening to the solemn words carried
on the chill air in the vicar's rather nervous voice. *I am
the resurrection and the life saith the Lord . . .*

He wasn't sure why he had come to the funeral of a
woman he had never actually met. Perhaps a polite wish to
pay his last respects given that, in a sense, he had been a
part of her death, if not her life? But it was rather more
than that, he thought. There was still the nagging feeling
that he owed her something more than respect; a feeling of
complicity with her. He had been the one to find her, the
one to whom she had seemed to want to speak.

From his vantage point on a slight rise in the ground, he could see the chief mourner at the graveside: a grim-faced Bruce King and, next to him but several feet apart, the son, Rex Farrell. A woman in grey stood beside the son, her face expressionless. No tears being shed there but there were plenty flowing among the theatrical crowd, playing their bit parts to the full. Any director would have approved.

Man that is born of a woman hath but a short time to live . . . he cometh up and is cut down like a flower . . .

Lois Delaney had certainly died before her time. She could have had a good many years ahead – years of useful life, as Dr Harvey had once told him firmly when he had first come to Frog End as a widower and had been feeling pathetically sorry for himself. She might have made a big come-back in *Hay Fever* – audiences were beginning to appreciate the old plays and recognize their worth. Bruce King might have been proved totally wrong in his predic-tion and Lois Delaney might have found a whole new career opening up before her. Except that, like the flower, she had been cut down.

The coffin was being lowered slowly into the ground.

Earth to earth, ashes to ashes, dust to dust . . .

Bruce King stepped forward with a single red rose in his hand which he let fall into the grave. Rex Farrell and the woman in grey scattered handfuls of earth.

Afterwards, the mourners stood around for a while and some of them threw more earth on to the coffin, rather dramatically. They began to drift away towards the lychgate where the hired coaches were waiting, together with newspaper photographers and a group of gawping villagers.

'I saw you in the church, Colonel. It was a lovely service, wasn't it?' Mrs Barnes, from the Hall, came up to him, dabbing at her red-rimmed eyes with a paper tissue. Her grief, he saw, was entirely genuine; she was not playing to any gallery or director.

'Yes, lovely.'

'Will you be going on to the hotel?'

'No, I don't think so.'

'I'd love to but Stanley wouldn't come to the service and I don't like to go on my own. I wouldn't have the nerve. Not with all these famous people . . . I've only ever seen them on the TV. It's quite a thrill to be seeing them in real life, and here in Frog End. I can't pretend it isn't, even though it's such a sad occasion.'

He realized that she was as overawed and star-struck as the vicar. 'Would you like me to accompany you to the hotel, Mrs Barnes?'

She looked at him gratefully. 'Would you really, Colonel? That's very kind of you.'

He escorted her to a coach and found places for them.

'The gentleman behind us,' she whispered. 'He's been in *Coronation Street*. And that one sitting two rows in front does the quiz show where they can win a million pounds. The girl beside him is his wife and she plays a nurse in the hospital soap.'

'Really?' He strove to look impressed.

The Chilcote Hotel was twelve miles or so from Frog End and set in many acres. The entrance gates, the colonel noticed, were brand new and similar in style to the gates at the Hall, only larger. The former stately home lay at the end of a long carriage drive – a magnificent Palladian building set against a backdrop of rolling Dorset hills. From a distance it seemed untouched by its transition but as the coach approached closer there were clear signs. The parkland where deer would once have grazed had become a golf course. The colonel could see the table-top flatness of the greens beneath the snow, the manmade hillocks of bunkers and what looked suspiciously like a man-excavated lake. A helicopter was parked close to the house – a gleaming silver and white machine and probably the preferred means of travel of most of the hotel's guests.

'That would belong to Mr King,' Mrs Barnes told him. 'He pilots it himself. Miss Delaney was terrified of flying in it.'

Naomi would have deplored both the helicopter and the

interior of the hotel, the colonel thought, as they went inside. The designer's makeover hovered somewhere between the Arabian Nights and a Venetian palazzo. Sumptuous wallpaper, heavily swagged drapes, dazzling crystal chandeliers, thick Turkish carpets on polished marble floors, sofas and armchairs to sink into in front of blazing log fires – real flames this time.

The wake refreshments were being served in what had probably been a ballroom – an enormous room with very tall windows overlooking the gardens at the back of the house. There were more crystal chandeliers glittering overhead and a deep-pile red carpet on the floor. The colonel fetched a cup of tea for Mrs Barnes from a side buffet. Waitresses came round with silver salvers of sandwiches and cakes, waiters with drinks. He took a whisky. Naomi would have grudgingly approved of the idea but not the rather small measure.

Among the crowd, he caught sight of Neville Avery with his companion. The doll-maker was chatting animatedly to another couple while the young man was standing a little apart, staring moodily at the carpet and saying nothing. Presumably they had met Lois Delaney at the Hall or elsewhere; Neville Avery struck him as the kind of man who would know a great many people.

He listened politely to Mrs Barnes pointing out more celebrities and thought how odd it was to see the famous in the flesh instead of on a stage or screen. They looked quite different. Shorter or taller, fatter or thinner, usually much older and more ordinary without the help of professional make-up and lighting. Very few had the stellar quality of someone like Lois Delaney; the special aura that dominated a scene and drew every gaze.

'Mrs Barnes . . . I'm so glad to see you here. How good of you to come.'

Lois Delaney's son, Rex Farrell, was shaking Mrs Barnes's hand and she was flushing with embarrassment.

'Well, I didn't quite know if I ought to be here, Mr Farrell.'

'But of course you should, Mrs Barnes. My mother would

have wished it. You were a great help and support to her at the Hall. She relied on you.'

'Thank you, sir.'

'Do you have everything you want, Mrs Barnes? Another cup of tea, perhaps? Some more cake?'

'No, thank you, sir. The colonel's kindly looking after me.'

A flashing smile in his direction. 'That's very good of you, Colonel.'

Rex Farrell could charm the birds out of the trees, the colonel thought drily, and probably did so regularly. He wondered if his court testimony had been anything like the whole truth. But it was commendable that he had taken the trouble to come over and speak to the caretaker's wife when his time might have been spent much more prof-itably cultivating the people in the room who could help get him some decent acting parts.

'I'm so sorry about your poor mother,' Mrs Barnes was saying. 'She was a lovely lady.'

'Yes, she was. Very lovely.'

'I'll miss her.'

'So will I, believe me. Very much. Tell me, Mrs Barnes, is there anyone here you'd specially like to meet? A favourite actor?'

Mrs Barnes flushed deeper. 'Well, sir, that gentleman over there – the one who plays the lawyer in that TV series. It'd be a such a thrill to meet him.'

He waved an imaginary wand. 'Your wish shall be granted, Cinderella. Come with me to the ball.'

The colonel watched as Mrs Barnes was escorted across the red carpet and introduced to the actor, who rose gallantly to the occasion. To his surprise, Rex Farrell then returned to his side.

'I remember you from the inquest, of course, Colonel. It must have been very unpleasant for you, finding my mother like that. You didn't actually know her, did you?'

He said, 'No. I'd only seen her on the stage.'

'It was a bit of a shock for me, I can tell you. She'd been on rather good form when I was with her at Christmas. Full of the joys, in fact. Talking non-stop about the play

– *Hay Fever*, you know. Magda was apparently very upbeat about it.'

'Magda?'

'Magda Dormon. Her agent. A fearful old dyke but she stuck by my mother for all the lean years. Did her level best for her when nobody else wanted to know any more. Then along comes this amazing offer. Noël Coward's back in favour, you see. The wheel's gone full circle. Audiences are getting tired of all the other stuff. They don't want to pay the earth to be made to think or worry. They want to be amused and entertained. My mother would have been perfect as Judith Bliss, of course.'

'I'm sure. It's a great pity her husband didn't see it that way too.'

'That's what I don't quite get. She never said anything to me about needing him to put up any money. And I'd have thought he'd have been the last person she'd ask. When he coughed up once before, the play folded after a week. And if there's one thing my stepfather doesn't like, it's losing money – not so much as a penny, and that was quite a lot of pennies. He made a great big fuss and when Bruce makes a fuss, it's not nice for anyone. I can't see her trying it again. As I understood it, the play already had backers anyway.'

'Oh, really?'

'Well, it's what my mama implied. It was a done deal. All ready to go. She'd even been learning the lines – acted out a scene when Jeanette came for a drink on Christmas Eve. Of course, she'd downed a few vodkas and kept bumping into the furniture, but she was word-perfect. She'd have wowed them, just like she always did.'

'I rather wondered whether the Bloody Marys might have got in the way? As your stepfather suggested in court?'

'Not a bit. Mama always followed Noël Coward's dictum to the letter: not a drop till the final curtain comes down.'

'So, she didn't mention writing to her husband and asking him to call at the Hall?'

'Not to me. The divorce was being handled through the lawyers and I can't imagine why she'd have wanted to see him. It was finished between them. Over and done with. Another of her mistakes, as she called it. The third one, unfortunately.'

'The marriage had been unhappy?'

'Not to begin with. I think she always started off in a sort of rosy glow of love and optimism. It just never lasted. I don't know much about her first marriage, but the second – to my father – was pretty good for a while, I think. The trouble was, he was an actor and not very successful – rather like me – and that's a recipe for disaster. The acting profession should never marry each other – it hardly ever works. Then, of course, she married Bruce. He'd been married twice before as well – did you know that?'

'No, I didn't.'

'He'd had a son by his first marriage, but he died of cystic fibrosis aged six. Then he got divorced and married again and divorced a second time. Neither of them had a very impressive track record in the matrimonial stakes. Mama was nearly five years older than him, but you'd never know it, and she was a pretty good wife to him. Worth her weight in gold. The glamorous hostess at all Bruce's boring business do's, entertaining useful contacts; out till all hours at dreary restaurants practically every night, buttering up the most ghastly types. She told me she had them all with their tongues hanging out, panting to sign on the dotted line. Of course, she missed the theatre like anything and in the end she got so bored and fed up that she went back on the bottle.'

'You didn't get on with your stepfather?'

Rex Farrell smiled. 'That's a bit of an understatement. I'm a no-good sponger, as far as he's concerned. He loathes me. I'm sure he's always thinking of the wonderful son that died and me undeservedly hale and hearty. It's perfectly true that my mother lent me money. We also had a rather good relationship and I think he was very jealous of that. I adored her – faults and all – and she was pretty fond of me. I came a fairly close second to the theatre.'

The colonel said slowly, 'And you had no reason to expect that your mother would try to take her own life?'

'On the contrary. As I said at the inquest, she was in high spirits over Christmas. Jeanette vouched for that.'

'I understand you've known Miss Hayes for some time?'

'About four years. We met at a party in London and I moved into the flat she rented the very next day. She finally threw me out last summer and I can't say I blame her. She works very hard and I'm a lazy bum. She got fed up with me lying about the place, doing nothing. Then a great-aunt died and left her some money, so she went off to live somewhere else. I'd no idea she was at the Hall till my mother told me. She was very fond of Jeanette. Always hoped we'd get back together, but there wasn't much chance of that.'

'Miss Hayes isn't here?'

'No, she's kept well away. Doesn't want to run into me again. Mama's twin turned up, though. That was a surprise.'

'Twin? I didn't realize she had one?'

'A twin sister. They weren't identical. In fact, they couldn't have been more different. My Aunt Iris is a schoolmarm. She was headmistress of a snobby girls' school in Wiltshire till she retired. She and my mother were never close. Their paths divided, as they say. Unlike Mama, Iris has never been married – not even once. She's standing over there, actually. Would you like to meet her?'

The colonel was presented to the woman in grey whom he had noticed at the funeral. As her nephew had said, she could hardly have been more different from Lois Delaney. Her hair was grey, like her drab clothes; she wore no make-up and her eyes were pale blue, not emerald green. An unidentical twin was merely a sibling, genetically speaking, but it still seemed extraordinary that the two should have inhabited the same womb at the same time.

She said, and in a very headmistressy voice: the voice of one accustomed to being in charge, 'I take it you're retired from the army, Colonel? Put out to grass, like me. Absurd the way they think we're no longer up to the job, isn't it?'

He agreed – certainly in her case. Iris Delaney looked perfectly capable of handling anything, mentally and physically.

She went on, 'I keep busy, of course. Committees, voluntary work . . . all that sort of thing, but it's only filling in time. Not the same thing at all.'

'No, indeed.' He couldn't see her joining the Venture for Retired People, unless it was to run it.

'Did you know my sister well, Colonel?'

He said apologetically, 'I'm afraid I'm here under false pretences, I didn't know her at all. I'd only seen her on the stage. I live in Frog End and happened to be calling at the Hall when she died.'

'So, you're the one who found her?'

'Yes.'

'How upsetting for you. I don't know why she chose such an unpleasant way to go. Pills were much more her style, washed down with plenty of vodka.'

'You weren't surprised that she took her own life?'

'Not really. I gather from Rex she'd nearly done it once before, six months ago. She had what people politely call a very fragile temperament. And I think she was, basically, an unhappy woman. She was famous and had had great success in her time, but her three marriages all failed and her star had faded.'

'She had been offered the chance for a come-back.'

Iris Delaney shrugged. 'Who knows if it would have worked? Bruce didn't think so, which is why he nipped it in the bud. Not very kind of him, but then he's not a very nice man. I never quite understood why Lois married him. He wasn't at all her usual type, but I suppose power and money can be attractive. My sister was always extremely extravagant, you see. Of course, she could afford to be when she was a big success but I expect the well had almost run dry by the time Bruce arrived on the scene.'

She waved away the platter of vol-au-vents thrust at her by a waiter. The colonel declined them too.

He said, 'Did you see much of your sister?'

'Practically nothing – once we were grown-up. Lois left school a year earlier than me and went more or less straight on to the stage. I stayed on and then went up to Oxford to read history. I became a teacher and, finally, a headmistress.' She looked at the colonel with a dry expression. 'As you can imagine, we lived in two different worlds. I used to go and see Lois in plays occasionally – she'd send me complimentary tickets – and once she came to present the drama cup at St Margaret's, but we were both preoccupied with our own lives and we had almost nothing in common. You seem very curious about my sister, Colonel, if you don't mind my saying so.'

'I'm sorry. It's none of my business, of course.'

'You needn't apologize. She often had that effect on people. They were fascinated by her. Drawn like moths to a bright flame. When she came into a room, everyone stopped talking and stared. Rather like with the Princess of Wales, I imagine. I was never envious of Lois – if that's what you're thinking. I would have hated her life. As I said, she wasn't very happy and although she knew a great many people, I don't think she was ever very close to any of them. Except for Rex, and one other person.'

'Oh?'

'Our old nanny. She would have been here today, but she's too frail now. Lois adored her. We both did, but Lois had a special rapport with her and Nanny Oliver helped look after Rex when he was born. After she retired Lois went to see her regularly for years but I'm ashamed to say I've only been a few times. My excuse is that a headmistress's life is very busy and Caister-on-Sea is a rather long way away from Hampshire. Do you know it, Colonel?'

'I'm afraid not.'

'It's in Norfolk. Nanny Oliver was born there – which is why she chose it. She bought a bungalow on the front but when she had a stroke last year, she had to move into an old people's home because she couldn't cope on her own any more. It's very sad when that happens, isn't it? Homes are such depressing places. Lois gave me the address and I sent a her a Christmas card and flowers, but I still haven't managed to get over to visit her. I feel very guilty about that.'

'Perhaps your sister went recently?'

'Oh, yes, I'm sure she would have done. She'd have gone to tell her about the divorce. She always told her everything. She used to say that Nanny still scolded her, but she always understood.'

The colonel thought of his own nanny who had never understood the first thing about the fierce military battles he had fought on the nursery floor with his toy soldiers, or the breakneck races he had run and won with his tinplate cars, or the complicated journeys undertaken with his train set. Nor had she ever appreciated how much he had hated broad beans and overcooked cabbage and bright yellow custard with wrinkled, leathery skin.

He said, 'I wasn't quite so lucky with mine.'

'Well, proper nannies scarcely exist any more, do they? People employ young foreign girls who are completely unknown, untrained and don't speak a word of English and they call them nannies and entrust their children to their care. Madness! The world is changing very fast around us, isn't it, Colonel? Everything is different: values, standards, communication, customs . . . But we have to move with the times, or be left high and dry.' She gave him a shrewd and unexpectedly humorous look. 'Don't we?'

He smiled at her. 'I'm afraid that's very true.'

'What are you sulking about *now*, Craig?'

'I'm not sulking, Neville.'

'Yes, you are, and it's very boring. I know this is a funeral but there's no need to look quite so miserable.'

'I don't much like these people. They're a bunch of tossers. Like they think they're God's gift.'

'They're in the theatre, dear boy. What else do you expect? They *are* God's gift, as they see it.'

'How come you know so many of them?'

'I already told you – I used to design theatre costumes, once upon a time.'

A snooty-looking waiter was shoving a plate of eats under their noses – bits of smoked salmon stuck on top of soggy crackers. Craig didn't think much of the food, nor did he think much of any of the waiters, or the waitresses either. They were all locals – he could tell that. Clumsy amateurs. Not a clue how to offer-up the plate, not a smile, no style. He could have done it loads better. The top-class waiters were always Italian or French and he'd been just as good as them in his day. He could have made a better job of the eats, too; not the same old stuff they were bringing out. You'd think a snob place like the Chilcote would do better, even if it was out in the middle of bloody nowhere.

Neville was talking to somebody else now and the two of them had their backs turned to him, like he wasn't worth bothering with. Sometimes, he wondered why he stayed. Maybe he wouldn't. Maybe he'd walk out one day. He could always find a job. He was a good enough cook now to earn his living at it instead of waiting tables. No need to stay where he wasn't appreciated. He didn't need an old queen like Neville, with his stupid dolls. He could find someone younger and better-looking, and with the dosh, too. There were plenty of them around, if you knew where to go.

He stared at Neville, gassing away to the other bloke. When he thought about it, he didn't know much about him at all – and not a thing about his past life. He'd never said a word about knowing Lois Delaney, for instance, which was weird, especially when she was living right next door to them. You'd think he'd've mentioned it, at least. And he hadn't told the cop that he'd left the flat that evening. Why hadn't he said something about that? He'd gone to ask Mr B to fix the work lamp, that's all, but, now that Craig thought about it some more, he'd taken a bloody long time about it when it'd only been a loose wire. Maybe he'd gone to see Lois Delaney as well? It must have been just after seven, if he remembered right, because he'd been in the kitchen starting the dinner, and Lois Delaney had died between six and eight. He knew that because the doctor bloke had said so in court when they'd gone to the inquest and that girl upstairs had said she'd knocked on the door of Flat 2 at half past seven and there hadn't been any answer, so the woman must have been dead already. Creepy!

That was another odd thing. Why had Neville wanted to go to the inquest, considering it was nothing to do with them? Bloody boring it had been, too. Worse than one of those operas.

He went on staring and thinking and wondering whether it wouldn't be a bloody good idea to push off and go back to London. And then just as he'd decided it would be and he was mentally packing his bags, Neville turned his head towards him and smiled.

'Is that you, Ruth?'

She recognized the voice at the other end of the wire – recognized it all too well.

'Yes. It's me.'

'It's Ralph here.'

'Hallo.'

'Just thought I'd give you a bell – see how you're getting on. It's ages since we met.'

Six months, to be precise. The last time she had seen him had been when she had been stupid enough to have lunch with him in London; when she had believed, against all the odds, that he was finally getting a divorce from his wife. The time when he had trotted out yet more excuses for waiting longer and shied away from giving her the help and support that she had desperately needed after Mama had been murdered.

'I'm fine, thanks.'

'Still living at the Manor, then.'

'Yes, I'm staying on for the time being.'

'Big place for you to run on your own.'

'Yes, it is, rather. But I manage.'

'Lonely, too.'

'Not really.' She tucked a strand of hair behind her ear and gripped the receiver more firmly. Cleared her throat. 'How are you, Ralph?'

'Well, things aren't too bright, as a matter of fact.'

'Oh?'

'Helen's left me. She walked out on Boxing Day.'

'I'm very sorry to hear that.'

'She wants a divorce. Apparently, she's met someone else.'

Oh, the irony! Their affair had lasted for eight years and she had lost count of the times he had sworn he was going to leave his wife and get a divorce. Now it was happening anyway.

'Isn't that what you wanted, Ralph? You always said so.'

'Yes, of course. I mean, Helen and I never really got along, as you know, but one stuck with it for the children's sake.'

And for the sake of a whole lot of other things, she thought. One reason trotted out after the other. But she couldn't blame him, she could only blame herself for getting involved with a married man in the first place and for staying involved in the second. But she had been so in love with him – so desperately in love that nothing else had seemed to matter.

He went on talking. He was a free man now. There was no reason why they shouldn't meet. As a matter of fact, he'd be down in Dorset next weekend, so perhaps he could come over to the Manor?

She thought as she stood there, clutching the receiver, it would be so easy to say yes, do come, Ralph. I'd love to see you, and it was true that she would. But she had known since their last meeting in London that she would never trust in him again. Never feel quite the same. She had finally succeeded in closing the door on their affair and she would be insane to reopen it. And yet, and yet . . .

'Ruth? Are you still there?'

'Yes, I'm here.'

'So, when shall I come?'

'Actually, I don't think it would be a good idea.'

He sounded very surprised – almost shocked. 'Why on earth not? There's nothing to stop us being together now.'

She said clearly, 'Yes, there is, Ralph. Me. I'm afraid I don't want to see you again. So, please don't ring any more.'

When she had put down the receiver she went into the drawing room and poured herself a large gin. That was that, then. Door firmly shut and bolted now. The end of the affair. At long, long last.

'I took you at your word, I'm afraid, Colonel. I hope you don't mind.'

'Not at all. Glad to see you.'

There was no car outside so Roy Ward must have walked over from the Hall with the express intention of calling at Pond Cottage, rather than dropping by in passing. It certainly wasn't the weather for a stroll and it had been dark for some time. The colonel took his coat and showed him into the sitting room where the curtains were drawn and the fire burning brightly. His visitor looked around with approval.

'This is how an English country cottage should be. What exiles in far away places dream of and long to come back to.'

'Didn't you say that you weren't so keen on that idea?'

'I wasn't, but my wife, Jean, was. Our flat at the Hall is very pleasant but it isn't a patch on this – in my opinion.'

'Nice of you to say so. The truth is that old cottages are the very devil to keep up. Draughts, damp, woodworm, dry rot . . . I wouldn't really recommend one. What'll you have to drink?'

'Whisky, if you have it.'

'Indeed, I do. A *stengah*?'

'How did you guess?'

'It used to be my tipple out in Malaya. An ideal drink in that climate. Water or soda?'

'Water, please.'

Thursday had opened one eye and stayed put. The colonel indicated the wing chair.

'Do sit down.'

He fetched the drinks – the long half-whisky, half-water *stengah* and his own a shorter version – and sat down at the other end of the sofa from Thursday, who shut his eye again.

Roy Ward said, 'You've even got a cat to go with the cottage.'

'I don't recommend him either. Good health!'

'Good health!'

'Your wife isn't back yet?'

'No, her sister's not doing too well, apparently. The doctors don't seem to be sure if the operation worked, or not. Something to do with the bone having deteriorated. My sister-in-law's a widow with no children, so there's nobody else to look after her. It looks like Jean's going to be away for quite a while.'

'Not so good for you – without her company.'

'That's true. It's all very different from Malaya. Well, you know what the social life out there was like. Something going on almost every night . . . nobody ever sat at home twiddling their thumbs, did they?'

'Not that I can remember.'

He and Laura had both thoroughly enjoyed their time in the Far East but he wasn't sure if he would have wanted to stay there for ever. Laura certainly wouldn't have done, any more than Jean Ward. She had always dreamed of living in a English country cottage. During one of their leaves, many summers ago, they had stopped at the spit-and-sawdust Dog and Duck at Frog End and sat on a bench in the sun outside the pub. Laura had pointed out the rose-covered cottage across the green and said that it was like her dream. They'd never got closer to the dream than a dreary flat in London before she had died. Afterwards, he had been staying with friends in Dorset in late autumn, and had driven round the countryside, trying to find the same place. He had finally found it, but the Dog and Duck had been transformed out of its spit-and-sawdust days,

and the cottage – Pond Cottage, without the roses in bloom
– had been nothing like as idyllic, close-up. As it happened,
it had been for sale and he had bought it against all sanity
and common sense and in spite of an appalling survey.
He had done so because it had been a part of Laura, if
only in a dream. While he lived in the cottage, she was
there, too, with him.

Roy Ward said, 'I wanted to ask your advice about something, as a matter of fact. I hope you don't mind.'

Strangely, people often did ask his advice and sometimes
about quite personal and private things; he had never felt
remotely qualified to give it. Maybe they imagined that he
must have had a lot of experience of life in the army. True
in some ways, but not in others.

'Ask away. I'll do my best.'

'It concerns Lois Delaney.'

'Oh?' His glass stopped in midair.

'I heard that it was you who found her body – on the
day when you came round collecting for that animal charity.'

'That's right.'

'Ghastly business! The police interviewed all the residents at the Hall of course – including myself. They asked
me if I knew her and I said that I didn't. That's not true,
of course. I met her at a party in Singapore many years
ago, before I knew Jean.'

'Yes, I remember you saying so. I thought it was rather
odd that when Inspector Squibb talked to me about the residents who had known Lois Delaney he didn't mention you.'

'Did you tell him about me?'

'No. There didn't seem any reason to. The inspector is
quite capable of conducting his own investigations.'

'The truth is that Lois Delaney and I had an affair.'

The colonel said slowly, 'It must have been something
to remember.'

'It was. I couldn't believe it was happening. I was head-
over-heels in love with her, of course – but so were lots of
other men. She had countless admirers in Singapore but,
for some reason, she chose me.'

'Perhaps she fell for you, too?'

'No . . . I don't flatter myself that was the case. But we spent three days together. I took her to an idyllic beach place I knew over on the Malay peninsula, right away from everything and everyone. It was paradise. Then, of course, we had to go back to Singapore and she left with the company to go on to Australia for the rest of their tour. I wrote letters to her and she answered. She went on writing back for a while but in the end, her letters petered out and, eventually, they stopped altogether. I never saw her again – at least, not until Jean and I came here. I'd no idea that she was living in a flat at the Hall but the caretaker happened to mention it one day. It was a hell of a shock, I can tell you. I'd never forgotten her, you see; carried a candle for her all those years. She was an exceptional woman – not only beautiful but utterly fascinating. When you were with her, you couldn't look at anything but her. Nothing and no one else existed.'

'I can well believe it.'

'Of course, I'd never mentioned the affair to Jean or even told her that I'd met Lois. There was no point and anyway it was something that I wanted to keep entirely to myself. I wanted to keep the memory of it unspoiled. Do you understand what I mean?'

'Completely.'

Some poetic lines came into the colonel's mind – something about memory painting a perfect day with colours that never fade. He knew of days and times like that.

Roy Ward gave him a grateful look. 'I thought you might.' He drank some of his *stengah*. 'I had no intention of bothering Lois, or of trying to see her. It's quite easy to keep oneself to oneself at the Hall – it's not a sociable kind of place. I expect that's one reason why she chose it. And, in any case, I doubted if she'd recognize me, if we did happen to meet by chance. I've changed quite a bit since my young days. And, of course, there was always Jean to consider. I didn't want her upset in any way.'

'Quite.'

'But then, when Jean went off to look after her sister after Christmas and I was left alone in the flat, I kept thinking

to myself, why the hell not? Why not at least say hallo?
There surely wouldn't be any harm in that? After all, it had
happened a long time ago and we were both getting on . . .
not like the young people we were. So, in the end, I went
down and knocked on her door.'

'When was this?'

'New Year's Eve, about four in the afternoon. I'd spent
most of the day trying to decide whether to do it or not,
getting up the nerve, I suppose.'

'And what happened?'

Roy Ward smiled ruefully. 'Nothing much. As I'd half-
expected, she didn't recognize me at all and she didn't even
remember my name. I could see that she'd been drinking
quite a bit – she had a Bloody Mary on the go – so at first
I thought it might be because of that, but then when I
reminded her about us meeting in Singapore and about the
beach paradise, she could hardly recall a thing about it. Oh,
she pretended to – just to be kind, I'm sure – but all she
really remembered was that *Blithe Spirit* had been a big
success there and how the audience had gone on and on
clapping for ten curtain calls. You can imagine how I felt.
My dream crumbled to dust.'

'You have my sympathy.'

'I don't deserve it. Going to see her was a lunatic thing
to do. Pathetic of me. Anyway, she was nice enough to offer
me a drink but I left after a short while. I knew I'd been a
complete fool – and that I'd been a fool for years. Then,
when the police told me the next day that she'd been found
dead, I'm afraid I didn't say anything about having known
her or about having seen her that afternoon. You see, the
inspector told me that her husband had called on her in the
evening and that she was still alive then, so I felt I was in
the clear, as it were. Even so, I was afraid of being impli-
cated somehow – made a suspect even – in which case Jean
would be bound to get to know all about it. She'd find out
that I'd gone down to the flat as soon as her back was
turned, and about my having an affair with Lois. I can tell
you that she wouldn't have taken it very well. So, I said
nothing and then when the coroner ruled that it was suicide,

there seemed even less reason to say anything. But, as time has gone by, I'm not so sure. Maybe I should come clean, as they say, and tell the police the whole story, even though it would make no difference to the verdict. It's been on my conscience. What do you think?'

The colonel took his time answering. Roy Ward's pride had been shattered, as well as his dream. Worse than rejecting him, Lois Delaney had forgotten him. She had not even remembered his name. The idyllic three days in Malaya when they had been lovers had very obviously meant little to her and were long forgotten. Men passionately in love had killed for less. But she had been alive when Bruce King had called later and, if Roy Ward had gone back to the flat afterwards with vengeance in his heart – which seemed most unlikely given the sort of man he was – then he would hardly have told him this tale or asked his advice.

He said slowly, 'I can't see any necessity to say any more to the police. A suicide verdict has been given, the case is closed. There seems little advantage in upsetting your wife.'

A sigh of relief. 'I'm very glad to hear you say that. Thank you.'

There was a real danger, the colonel thought somewhat grimly, of landing himself in all kinds of trouble for conspiring to withhold evidence in a police investigation. First Miss Butler – twice over – and now Roy Ward. Who would be next? He drained his glass and stood up.

'Time for the other half, I think. We could both do with it.'

'I could indeed.'

When he had refilled the glasses and sat down again, the colonel said, 'By the way, when you saw Lois Delaney that afternoon, what sort of mood was she in? Did she seem down in the dumps? Depressed?'

'Not at all. Far from it. As I said, she'd obviously drunk quite a bit but she was in a happy mood, not in the least maudlin. She told that she was returning to the West End at long last and how thrilled she was. That was really all she wanted to talk about. The theatre and the play. She didn't seem to care about anything else.' Roy Ward downed more of his *stengah* and looked at the colonel. 'Of course, I know you'll keep our conversation to yourself.'

That was another thing, the colonel thought, bemused. People always assumed that they could trust him implicitly to keep their secrets. It never seemed to occur to them that he might do otherwise. Perhaps that was why they picked on him in the first place.

Ten

'Good morning, Colonel. Hope I'm not disturbing you too early?'

Ruth Swynford stood on his doorstep, arms full of a large, newspaper-wrapped bundle. Her cheeks and the tip of her nose were pink from the cold.

'Not a bit. Come in, quickly, before you freeze to death.'

'I've got snowy boots on.'

'My hallway doesn't mind that any more than your flag-stones did.'

She stepped inside. 'Some hellebores for you. Naomi said you ought to have some to cheer you up but you look quite cheerful to me.'

He smiled. 'I am. But it's very good of you to bring them. How much do I owe you?'

'Nothing. I had too many of them. You'll be doing me a favour by taking them off my hands. I need the space.'

He didn't really believe her but he knew it would be pointless, as well as ungracious, to argue. 'What do I do with them?'

'You needn't do anything till the snow goes. I've put them in pots so they won't mind waiting around; you can plant them out when you're ready. Naomi's earmarked a spot in your garden, but don't let her bully you. They're already flowering. Look.'

She lifted a corner of the newspaper and he peered at the pure white buds – one or two of them already open.

'They're beautiful.'

'Yes. It's a pity they're so bashful. They hang their heads and you have to make them look up to see them properly.' She raised a cup-shaped bloom gently with one finger and he admired the delicate purple splashes around its green and yellow centre. 'Some people plant them on a bank so they can see them better, but Naomi says you haven't got one.'

'They'll give me great pleasure. Thank you, Ruth.'

'You're welcome.'

'I'll put them on the kitchen table for the time being.'

He carried the bundle through and she followed him.

'Did you go to Lois Delaney's funeral, by the way, Colonel?'

'Yes, I did, as a matter of fact.'

'I don't think the village has ever seen anything like it before. I hope people don't start making pilgrimages to her grave and leaving those depressing bunches of flowers.'

'I think that's unlikely.'

'Poor woman. I felt quite sorry for her. She must have been really miserable to want to kill herself. I once felt like that. Life didn't seem worth living and then, when my mother was murdered, it seemed even worse. Do you remember how the police suspected me at first, before they found the real culprit?'

'Yes, I do. A very unhappy time for you.'

She didn't know it – nobody did, or ever would, except the murderer – but he had been instrumental in solving the crime.

'Tom Harvey doesn't think she did kill herself.'

'Oh? Why doesn't he?'

'He said she had something to live for.'

'It would seem so.'

'I hear they held the wake at that posh country hotel. The place the millionaire husband owns.'

'It's not posh exactly,' he said. 'And I don't think you'd like it very much, Ruth.'

She smiled. 'I'm not sure they'd let me in anyway. Not dressed like this.'

He saw her back to the front door where she paused; he noticed that her pink cheeks had gone even pinker.

'By the way, Tom Harvey has asked me to marry him. I

wondered what you'd think of the idea, Colonel? I'd value your opinion.'

Here we go again, he thought: someone else asking me about something very personal. In Ruth's case, it was probably because of his grey hairs and because she had no father to ask.

He said firmly, 'I think Tom Harvey is a very fine young man as well as a very fine doctor. And I think you'd be very happy together.'

She nodded. 'I thought you'd probably say that. Everybody likes Tom. I do, too. Very much. It's just that I'm still a bit gun-shy, if you know what I mean. There was someone else for a long time and it's only just ended. I don't feel ready for anything else yet.'

'I understand. He'll want an answer, though, sooner or later.'

'That's the trouble. He says if it's "no", he'll leave Frog End. Go off somewhere miles away – America or Australia, somewhere like that.'

'Which would be a great pity.'

'Yes, it would, wouldn't it? The village needs him. I'd hate to feel responsible for him going.'

The colonel smiled to himself. Dr Harvey was not above a bit of cunning blackmail. He'd have tried the same in his shoes, if it worked.

After Ruth had gone he opened up the newspaper bundle. The hellebores sat there shyly and he lifted a flower under the chin so that he could admire its beauty again.

'Don't worry,' he told his newcomers. 'You'll soon settle in. I'm going to plant you near the back door so I can keep an eye on you through the window. We can't have you blushing unseen.'

It was just as well, he thought drily, that there was nobody, except Thursday, to hear him.

Around midday the colonel took a walk around the green and stopped in at the Dog and Duck. The pub was almost empty. Sheila, the landlady was polishing glasses and Major

Cuthbertson, who must have slipped his leash, was sitting morosely at the bar in front of a near-empty glass of whisky.

The colonel said, 'Good to see you about again, Major. Will you have the other half?'

'I wouldn't say no. Best medicine there is.'

'I quite agree.'

He ordered two doubles and then raised his glass.

'Happy New Year to you.'

The major grunted. 'Nothing very happy about it so far.' He tossed back the dregs in his glass and started on the next. 'Bad business about Miss Delaney.'

'Indeed, it is.'

'Mind telling me what happened, exactly?'

The colonel gave an abridged account.

Major Cuthbertson took another gulp. 'Damned unfortunate – all those policemen gawping. A woman like that.'

'I agree.'

'Knew you would. I met her once, as a matter of fact.'

'Did you really?'

'Years ago. We had quite an understanding.' He tapped the side of his nose. 'Mum's the word, though.'

'Of course.'

'Marjorie can get pretty jealous.'

The colonel kept a straight face. 'I won't tell her, I promise.'

The major took another swig. 'God knows why someone like her would want to do herself in. Doesn't make any sense at all.'

No, he thought. It doesn't.

'Got down in the dumps, I suppose. Like we all do. Felt the same myself. Still, there was no need to go and do a thing like that. Bit drastic, wasn't it? I mean, there's no going back. No changing your mind. Damned shame!'

He bought the major another whisky before he went on his way back to the cottage. As he was nearing the gate, Tom Harvey drove past, slowed his car to a stop and lowered the window.

'How are things, Colonel?'

'Pretty good, thanks.'

The young doctor was the near-extinct sort of GP who took a real interest in his patients. If he left Frog End it would, indeed, be a sad loss but, somehow he didn't think that was going to happen. Ruth would eventually give in.

'I saw you at the inquest, Colonel. Bad luck finding the body. Getting dragged into it. It can be a lot of hassle.'

'It certainly can.'

'I remember I was once travelling in a train, coming back from a medical conference in Wales, and some man in the compartment died. He was sitting bolt upright, stone dead, and nobody seemed to notice. I did, though, and so did three other doctors in the same compartment. I'm ashamed to say we all sneaked off the train without saying a word to anyone. None of us wanted to get involved in all the hoo-ha.'

The colonel smiled. 'Perfectly understandable.'

'Very unprofessional though. Don't tell our Inspector Squibb. He'd have me clapped in irons.'

He said, 'By the way, Ruth told me you didn't think Lois Delaney killed herself. I thought that was interesting.'

'Yes, I remember saying so. But what do I know, Colonel? I'm just a humble GP.'

'I would have thought you knew quite a lot. You're in the front line. You see it all. Lots of first-hand experience of how people behave.'

'Well, the experts thought she did. We have to assume they know better. Better press on, Colonel. Duty calls.'

Tom Harvey waved and drove off.

The colonel went into Pond Cottage thoughtfully; he didn't assume anything of the kind.

The helicopter made a deafening racket as it descended towards the lawn. Jeanette threw down her paintbrush and put her hands over her ears. She got up from the stool and went over to the attic window. The helicopter was hovering just above the ground, propellers whirring, snow blowing around in great flurries. As she watched, it finally touched down and the noise died away.

What horrible machines they were! Noisy, ugly, clumsy

with none of the grace of proper aeroplanes. But it had to be admitted that they had their uses in emergencies. Ferrying people to hospital, snatching them off sinking ships and from cliff faces and the tops of mountains and the middle of deserts. And, of course, they made ordinary journeys far quicker and easier. No traffic jams; no being stuck in long tail-backs for hours on motorways. A to B in the fastest time possible, which is why very rich, important and busy people used them.

After a moment, the helicopter's door opened and Bruce King climbed out of the pilot's seat. Lois had told her that he always insisted on flying the machine himself, even though he could have afforded a tame pilot. Some sort of macho thing probably. Lois had flown in it once and never again; she had been scared stiff.

She watched him walk across the lawn towards the drive and the front door. Walk wasn't the word: stride was better. He probably strode everywhere, barking out orders to assistants and underlings. She had only met him once during the time she had lived with Rex. Lois had invited them to dinner – which had been a big mistake. Bruce had made no effort to conceal his feelings about Rex and he had barely troubled to speak a word to her. They had left as soon as possible and she hadn't seen him again until the inquest into Lois's death.

It was a mystery why Lois had ever married him. The obvious reason was for the money but she didn't think that had been the case. Lois had certainly liked spending it, but she'd been no gold-digger. Neither of her first two husbands had been well off and it had been Lois who had earned the real bread in those days. Perhaps when she'd stopped earning as much, it had been a relief to hand over to somebody else with bottomless pockets.

Bruce King had disappeared around the corner, out of sight. Presumably, he would have come to see about Flat 2, to go through everything and arrange for it to be put back on the market. He was a businessman, first and foremost, as he had declared at the inquest, making no bones about it. Miss Quinn, of course, would be hanging over the banisters like a vulture, waiting to see what went on.

She went back to the plate and the painting of two blue-birds on a branch. She'd had to look them up in her *Illustrated Birds of the World* book because there were no bluebirds in England, in spite of the old wartime song about them being over the white cliffs of Dover. They were North American birds – quite big ones, seven inches long, with a blue back and blue tail feathers and a reddish breast.

She went on working for an hour or more before she heard the helicopter start up again. There was another deafening racket and, from her stool, she saw it rise up slowly past the window and fly away.

She had finished the plate by the end of the morning and was washing her brushes when the flat doorbell rang. When she opened the door, Rex was standing there. He stuck his foot quickly in the gap before she could shut it again.

'I'd like to talk to you, Jeanie. I promise not to stay long.'

He was leaning his whole weight against the door, as well as keeping the foot in the gap. She shrugged and let go.

'You may as well come all the way in.'

He did, and stood looking down at her. In spite of herself, she felt the old attraction. The look was just as heart-melting, his pet name for her just as affecting.

She said coolly, 'What the hell are you doing here, Rex?'

'I came to see if I could get into Mama's flat.'

'What for?'

'I wasn't intending to loot the place, so there's no need to look at me like that. She happened to have albums of old family photos that I'd quite like to have – pictures of her with me as a child – that sort of thing. Sentimental value. And some rather good studio portraits of her in her younger acting days which I rather like.'

'Well, they belong to you now, don't they?'

'I have a moral right to them, you could say. Unfortunately, I can't get into the flat to remove them.'

'Mrs Barnes will let you in.'

'No, she won't. Brucie has left strict orders that nobody is to go in there, especially not me. She said she's very sorry but those were his instructions. Poor woman, she was quite upset about it.'

'He was here a while ago. Came in his helicopter.'

'Yes, Mrs Barnes told me. I'm probably too late.'

'But surely he'd let you have the photos? They're not worth anything to him.'

'Not a hope. He'd sooner bin them, shred them or send them off to the dump. You know how he feels about me.'

'What about your mother's will? She might have left them to you specifically. She'd have wanted you to have them.'

'She never made a will. Couldn't bear the thought of doing one. Much too morbid for her. And she was still married to Bruce, so he gets everything. Not that she had much cash left in the bank, but, as I say, it's the photos that I really mind about.'

She knew him well enough to see that he was telling the truth. He *did* mind. And she could understand it perfectly. Photographs of people you loved, or had loved, were beyond price and irreplaceable. If your home burned down, you could always get new carpets and televisions and furniture with the insurance, but you could never replace the photographs. They were gone for ever. When her mother had died after a horrible, lingering illness, her father had re-married within a year and her stepmother had thrown out all the precious old family photos, including a lovely studio portrait of her mother. It still hurt to think about it. Still made her furiously angry.

She said slowly, 'Would you like me to try and get them, Rex? I might be able to persuade the Barnes's to let me in . . . to think of some excuse.'

'No chance. It'd be more than their job's worth, Mrs B said. Bruce would have them out on their ear.'

'We certainly wouldn't want to risk that.' She frowned, thinking. 'I might be able to get hold of the key. The Barnes's keep them on hooks in their hallway. I've seen them there.'

He looked at her for a moment and then smiled. 'Would you really do that for me, Jeanie?'

'Not for *you* exactly, Rex. I just don't like the thought of your stepfather throwing the photos away. It wouldn't be fair. Tell me where she kept the albums.'

'On the bookshelves in the sitting room. There are about six or more of them – all bound in blue leather. She always used to buy them from the same place in Bond Street.'

'And the studio ones?'

'Dotted all over the place. Silver frames mostly.'

She nodded. 'I remember them. I'll see what I can do.'

'Thanks.'

He took a step forward and she took two back.

'Well, what else did you want to talk to me about, Rex?'

'Anything I could think of. To see if there was the slightest chance of us getting back together again.'

'None at all, Rex.'

'That's a great shame.'

'No, it isn't. It's a very good thing. I've got my life together now and I don't want you around any more.'

'Harsh words, Jeanie. As a matter of fact, I was going to tell you that I've been getting mine together too. Rather well actually. I've just landed a part in a new TV cop series.'

'PC Plod?'

'Nothing plodding about it. I'm the star detective. You know the type – divorced, ruthless, rude to everyone, lives on his own, drinks too much. They think I'll turn-on all the female viewers.'

'Congratulations. But you don't turn *me* on any more, Rex. So there's no point coming here again.'

'Well, it was worth a try.'

'So, if that's all, I've got work to do.'

He went to the flat door and opened it. 'Do you realize, Jeanie, that if my beloved Mama had topped herself *after* the divorce and settlement, I'd have collected twenty million pounds as her sole heir? Whether my stepfather liked it or not.'

'You still wouldn't have turned me on, Rex. And the money would have been the ruin of you.'

He grinned. 'You're probably quite right. But just think how it would have pissed old Brucie off.'

*   *   *

The colonel switched on the record player and settled down comfortably in his wing chair to listen to *The Pirates of Penzance*.

> *With cat-like tread,*
> *Upon our prey we steal;*
> *In silence dread,*
> *Our cautious way we feel.*
> *No sound at all!*
> *We never speak a word;*
> *A fly's foot-fall*
> *Would be distinctly heard . . .*

Blast it! He still couldn't get Lois Delaney out of his head. She was in there, interfering with his enjoyment of the music, distracting him from the simple pleasure of the familiar words. He ejected her firmly.

The chapter was closed. There had been a police inquiry, an inquest, a verdict, a funeral, an end to it all. Any crazy idea he had had about her wanting to communicate something to him had been entirely fancy – the overactive imagination of a foolish old man.

He went on listening.

> *So stealthily the pirate creeps,*
> *While all the household soundly sleeps.*

The phone rang suddenly and he sighed and got up to turn down the volume and answer it.

'Dad? Thank God you're there!'

His son's voice sounded desperate.

'What is it, Marcus? Has something happened?'

'I've just come back from the hospital. Susan was rushed there in an ambulance. It's a threatened miscarriage.'

'I'm very sorry to hear that.'

'It doesn't look too good at the moment. So far she's held on to the baby, but they're keeping her in and they say she'll have to be in there for several days – maybe a week or more. She was in quite a state, as you can imagine.'

Yes, he could. 'I'm sure everything will be all right, Marcus. Try not to worry too much. They'll save the baby if they possibly can.'

'The trouble is, Eric has to be looked after. Our neighbour's been taking care of him today but I can't leave him with her any longer – she has to go to work tomorrow. And I can't take much time off myself – we're terribly busy at the office. We're launching a new kind of pasta next week. Big promotion, national press, all that sort of thing.'

'Sounds exciting.'

'It is, and I've simply got to be there.'

'Is there anyone else who could look after him? A friend? Another mother?'

'Not really. The trouble is we haven't lived here very long so Susan hasn't made any real friends yet, and she doesn't like leaving Eric with people she doesn't know well. Do you think you could have him, Dad? Just for a few days? I could drive him down tomorrow – the main roads are more or less clear now. I'll bring all his kit – clothes, toys, books and everything.'

The colonel felt his heart plummet. He had tried, since his grandson had been born, to care about him but, so far, he had failed. The child wasn't responsible for inheriting his mother's looks – the pale skin, wispy hair and gooseberry eyes – but they were not helped by his constant whingeing and whining and his frequent temper tantrums. His daughter-in-law maintained that the boy was highly strung and had taken him to a psychologist to prove it. Allowances, apparently, had to be made, though his own fingers had often itched to administer a sound slap instead.

'Would that be OK, Dad?'

'Yes, of course. I'd be delighted to have him. Glad to help.'

'That's wonderful.' Marcus sounded relieved. 'I'll bring him tomorrow morning. We ought to be with you around lunchtime. How are the local roads?'

'Still snowy but passable. You'll need to take care. Watch out for patches of ice.'

'I will.'

'By the way, what would Eric like to eat for lunch, do you think?'

'Oh, I don't know. Anything you've got.'

He put the phone down, his heart still at boot level. He could remember the violent arguments at meal times, food flying, spoons flung to the floor, shrieks and wails. After a moment, he reached for the phone again and dialled Naomi's number. When she answered he said simply: 'SOS.'

She came round at once, tipped Thursday off the sofa, took his place and accepted a large glass of Chivas Regal with a small splash of water.

'So, what's all the panic, Hugh?'

He told her, 'I'm not sure I can cope.'

'When does the little bugger arrive?'

'Around lunchtime tomorrow. What on earth am I going to give him to eat? He's extremely picky.'

'We'll think of something.' Naomi took a gulp from her glass. 'How old did you say he was?'

'He'll be five later this year.'

'Hmmm. Not an easy age. Well, you must start as you mean to go on, Hugh. No good pandering to him. You've got to take the upper hand from the word go.'

'Easier said than done; he's very spoiled.'

'You're an army man, Hugh. You've commanded grown men. Given them orders and generally bossed everyone around.'

'I'm not in the army any more, Naomi. I'm a grandfather who doesn't have the faintest idea how to look after a small child. Laura always dealt with all that.'

She gave him a grim smile. 'Time you learned, Hugh.'

As with the garden, Naomi resorted to paper and pencil to make one of her plans of action.

'Shopping list: baked beans, fish fingers, oven chips, ice-cream, frozen peas . . .'

He looked over her shoulder, seeing some classic Naomi spellings – *spagetty hoops, beefbergers, chicken nuggets, fruit yoggurts, frozen stake and kidney pie.*

'I thought you disapproved of all that sort of junk food, Naomi?'

'I do, but this is an emergency. You'll have your hands full looking after that boy, keeping him out of mischief. No time to spend fiddling around in the kitchen, and no point if he's such a fuss-pot.'

'What about lunch tomorrow?'

'That's what the steak and kidney's for. Your son will need feeding too after driving all that way, and he won't want the kids' stuff.'

'Supposing Eric won't eat it?'

'Then the little perisher can go without.' She took another swig. 'Now, things to do.'

'What do you mean exactly?'

'You'll have to entertain him, Hugh. Keep him amused. Snakes and ladders, puzzles, Lego, colouring books, crayons. Have you got any of those?'

'I'm afraid not.'

'Well, you'll need to get them. Woolworths toy department in Dorchester is the place to go. And, you'll have to take him out.'

'Will I?'

'Of course. You won't want to stay cooped up in the cottage all day and the roads aren't too bad now. There's the cinema in Dorchester – if there's anything suitable on. And you could take him to the Military Museum, though he might find looking at uniforms and medals a bit boring at his age. And you could go over to Maiden Castle. It's a good place for kids to run around and let off steam.'

The colonel said suddenly, 'There's always Bovington.'

'Bovington?'

'Tanks,' he said, brightening considerably. 'Army tanks. There's a museum there too.'

There was no time to lose, Jeanette decided. Bruce could send people to clear out the flat at any time, or he might come back himself. She went downstairs and rang at the Barnes's door.

Mr Barnes opened it. Mrs Barnes had, apparently, taken the bus to Dorchester to do some shopping, which was a piece of luck because he would be much easier to deal with.

She smiled brightly at him. Would it be possible to borrow a tin opener – just for a few minutes? Hers had just broken.

He went away to fetch one from the kitchen. The keys were exactly where she remembered – hanging in a row on the wall in the hallway and clearly numbered. She took No. 2 off its hook and put it in her pocket before the caretaker returned with the tin opener.

'I'll bring it back soon, Mr Barnes, I promise.'

'No need to rush, miss,' he said. 'Take your time.'

Miss Quinn wasn't at her snooping post for once, and there was nobody else about to see her let herself very quietly into the flat. The scent that Lois had always worn still hung poignantly on the air. She stood in the hallway for a moment, wondering why she was doing this and what on earth she would say if she were caught.

The curtains in the sitting room were half-drawn, the light dim, but she dared not risk turning on any of the lamps. She went straight to the bookcase and found the set of albums – there were six of them and they were heavy. She unfolded the black bin liner she had brought with her, put them in and moved some of the other books along to fill the gap. Then she went around the room, collecting up framed photographs – mostly of Lois but some were of Rex. There were more in the bedroom and she snatched those up too. She left some behind – a clean sweep would have been too obvious and too risky.

The door to the bathroom was ajar and she couldn't help peering inside and looking at the bath where Lois had died. The Wiberg's pine essence that she had always sworn by was on a shelf. She shivered.

She carried the bin liner out of the flat and upstairs to the attic. Luck was with her again. No Miss Quinn appeared, nor did anybody else.

As soon as she had dumped the bin liner, she went back down and returned the tin opener. More luck: Mrs Barnes was still out shopping.

'I'm sorry to be such a nuisance,' she said to the caretaker. 'But could I possibly take a look at your local phone book while I'm here? I can't seem to find mine anywhere.'

While he was gone she put the key back on its hook and when he returned with the phone book, she pretended to look up a number.

'Shall I write it down for you?' he asked helpfully.

'No, thanks. I can remember it.'

Back in the attic, she sat down and took some deep breaths to steady herself. It had been easy – much easier than she had expected. Nothing had gone wrong and no one had seen her.

As she sat there, recovering, it suddenly occurred to her how easy it would have been for the Barnes's to go in and out of Flat 2 at any time they pleased, and with a multitude of excuses: cleaning, maintenance, odd jobs for Lois. She frowned. Everybody believed that Lois had killed herself, but Rex, who probably knew his mother better than anyone, had had no reason to expect it. *None whatsoever.* That's what he'd said at the inquest. And Lois had been in such good form on Christmas Eve. She'd waltzed around the room, acting out a scene from *Hay Fever* and doing it wonderfully. Supposing the Barnes's had had some sort of grudge against Lois? Supposing she'd threatened to get them fired because of something they'd done? Perhaps they'd stolen something? Or been caught snooping through drawers? Supposing one of them had gone in there, knowing very well she was taking a bath, and then chucked the hairdryer into the bath?

Jeanette stopped supposing anything of the kind. It was all too far-fetched and ridiculous. The Barnes's were decent people and they'd both been very upset at Lois's death – especially Mrs Barnes.

She got up and went into her bedroom where she'd left the bin liner.

She sat on the bed and took out the silver framed studio portraits.

Beautiful studies of Lois when she had been at the height of her stardom, taken by a famous London society photographer – softly lit and flattering, looking upwards, or with her head tilted, or with her chin resting on a hand. The ones of Rex had been taken by the same photographer and they were pretty flattering too. Rex aged about four, all togged up in satin ruffles as an angelic pageboy; Rex as a teenager in his public school uniform – already promising the good looks and the charm; Rex as a young grown-up man in a Savile Row lounge suit – smiling and impossibly handsome.

And what about Rex if it came to supposing things? He'd said he was driving up to Scotland for a New Year's Eve party, but that he'd got stuck in the snow and had to spend most of the night in the car. But supposing he'd lied about it – she'd known him tell plenty of lies if it suited him. Perhaps he'd come back to the Hall? To kill his own mother? That was nonsense, too. He'd adored her. And, besides, what would he want to kill her for? If twenty million pounds was the motive then he'd have waited until *after* the divorce. He'd pointed that out himself. Made quite a point of it, in fact.

She took out one of the blue leather albums. Family snaps taken in summery gardens, on tennis courts and croquet lawns, on beaches, on picnics . . . happy days. Jeanette sat there for a long time, slowly turning the pages.

Ruth was busy sewing seeds in one of the greenhouses when Tom Harvey appeared. There was no chance of doing a bunk because he was standing firmly between her and the door and he didn't do any beating about the bushes either.

'I've come for your answer, Ruth.'

She straightened up, pushing her hair off her face. 'I can't give you one yet, Tom. I'm awfully sorry.'

'And I can't wait much longer.'

'You mean you'll leave Frog End?'

'If you turn me down – yes. I don't want to hang about if you're still in love with somebody else.'

She flushed. 'I'm not . . . not any more.'

'But you're not in love with me?'

'Well, no . . .'

'Why not give it a try?'

'I've got a lot on my mind, just at the moment.' She

waved a hand around the greenhouse – at the seed trays, the cuttings, the young plants. 'Getting going with all this. I can't think about anything else. I need time.'

'How much do you need?'

'I don't know. Whatever it takes.'

'That's no good, Ruth. You can't keep me dangling on the end of a string indefinitely.'

'I won't. Anyway, after my mother died you said you'd be around. Like the song says.'

'I can't stay around for ever. Not unless you marry me.'

'You mean you'll go off to America?'

'Or maybe Australia. I've always had a hankering to see what it's like living upside down.'

'They're both a very long way away.'

'Yes, they are. That's the whole point.'

She looked at him unhappily, not knowing what to say. She had come to depend on him much more than she had realized: used him as a sort of prop, while keeping him at arm's length – which hadn't been fair, of course. He'd every right to issue a sort of ultimatum. But Frog End would miss him badly. He was a wonderful doctor – marvellous with children and the elderly, marvellous with everybody, in fact. She'd seen him in action, crouching down to talk to a child at its own level, putting a steadying hand on the shoulder of a young man condemned to spend the rest of his life in a wheelchair, making a sick old man roar with laugher. It would be dreadful if he left. And it would be her fault.

'I'll think harder about it, I promise.'

'That's the spirit.' He turned to open the greenhouse door. 'By the way, you've got dirt all over your forehead.'

She rubbed at it with her hand. 'I always get filthy working.'

He smiled. 'You've made it worse now.'

He was worth ten of Ralph, she thought, staring after him through the greenhouse glass. No, not ten – twenty. No – thirty, forty, fifty at least, and probably a great deal more.

Eleven

Marcus arrived at Pond Cottage just before two. The colonel had progressed from being vaguely uneasy about his arrival to starting to worry in earnest, when his son's car drew up outside the front gate. He hurried out to greet him.

'Sorry, Dad. Some of the roads were pretty icy and the traffic on the motorway was hellish. And then Eric was sick so I had to stop and clean him up. I'm afraid he's still in a bit of a mess.'

'Don't worry. We'll deal with it. Glad you're here safely. That's all that matters.'

He peered in through the car window. Eric was strapped in his child's seat in the back, his pale face even paler and blotched unattractively with tears. His red anorak was smeared with vomit and he was clutching his toy rabbit tightly by the ear.

The colonel said encouragingly, 'We'll soon have you out of there, old chap.'

His grandson snivelled as Marcus unstrapped him and lifted him out of the car.

'Could you take him inside, Dad? I'll bring all the stuff.'

'Come on, Eric.'

Eric scowled and turned away. Remembering Naomi's words, he took hold of the child's hand firmly and, more or less, dragged him indoors. When he tried to remove the sick-covered anorak, the zip stuck halfway but he managed to get it off over Eric's head and past the rabbit, still attached to Eric's hand, down one sleeve. There was more vomit, he noticed, over Eric's trousers. His grandson started to howl as Marcus appeared, laden with suitcase and plastic bags and bundles and the car seat.

'He's in a bit of a state, one way and another. You can't blame him.'

'Of course not, the poor chap. I expect he feels rotten. What can I do to help?'

'Well, I think the best thing would be for us to get him to bed for a bit. If he sleeps, he'll feel better.'

Between them they got Eric, the rabbit and the suitcase up the stairs and into the small spare room. Surprisingly, the boy lay down without any argument and shut his eyes. They went downstairs.

'You'll have some lunch, Marcus? It's ready.'

'If you don't mind, Dad, I think I'll push off straight away. I ought to get back so I can go and see Susan. She's pretty upset. I'll grab a sandwich when I stop for petrol.'

'Will Eric want anything to eat, do you think?'

'I doubt it. I'd leave him to sleep as long as possible. He might fancy something later.'

'What sort of thing?'

'Oh, fruit. Cereal. Nothing rich.'

When Marcus had gone, the colonel put the anorak and the trousers into the washing machine and sat alone, eating his steak and kidney pie and peas. After a few mouthfuls, he pushed them away.

Susan phoned from her hospital bed in the evening, sounding very weak.

'How is Eric, Father? I've been so worried about him.'

'He's fine, Susan. He's sitting watching television at the moment.'

A game of snakes and ladders had ended in sulky tears when Eric had gone down the longest snake near the end, right back to the beginning, and an attempt at a jigsaw puzzle had failed equally dismally with pieces being thrown about the sitting room – some of them deliberately aimed at Thursday, who had hissed and spat furiously from the sofa. In desperation, the colonel had turned on the television.

'I don't ever let him see anything scary. It could give him nightmares.'

'It's only *The Simpsons*.'

'Oh, dear . . . he's not supposed to watch that. I think it's an awful programme. Very vulgar.'

He looked across at his grandson, whose eyes were fixed on the screen. 'I won't let him watch it again.'

'He ought to go to bed soon.'

'He's all ready for it. He's had a bath and he's in his pyjamas and dressing-gown.'

There had been a big drama over that, too – Eric refusing to get in the bath, then refusing to get out; finally, the colonel had hauled him out bodily, the child struggling and screaming.

'Did you make him put his slippers on?'

Another white lie. The colonel had forgotten to unpack them. 'Oh, yes.'

'Has he had some supper?'

'He wasn't very hungry. I gave him cornflakes and yoghurt. He seemed to like them all right.' He hadn't offered anything else.

'*Organic* yoghurt?'

'Oh, yes,' he lied again. No point in upsetting her, not in her condition.

'Because his digestive system's very sensitive.'

Eric had eaten three of the luridly coloured and highly inorganic yoghurts, apparently without ill effect, so far.

'He seems quite all right.'

'Marcus should have told you that he only drinks soya milk. Anything else brings him out in a rash.'

'I'll get some tomorrow,' he promised.

'You will be careful what you give him, won't you, Father? I never let him have any of those awful junk foods – burgers or nuggets or chips – they're so bad for children. And chocolate makes him hyperactive.'

'I'll remember that.'

'And he must wear his hat and scarf and gloves if he goes out, or he might catch a chill.'

'I'll see that he wears them.'

Her voice quavered. 'It's very kind of you, Father. I'm very grateful.'

He said gently, 'It's no trouble. How are you feeling, Susan?'

'A bit better. They seem to think the baby might be all right, but I've got to stay in bed for several more days.' She gulped. 'I do miss Eric.'

'Well, you mustn't worry about him. He'll be fine. We're going to do some things together. Go on some outings.'

He didn't mention the tanks in case they were banned too.

The colonel drove over to Bovington through the snow, his grandson slumped sullenly in the child's seat in the back. There were some icy patches here and there, but he went slowly and carefully. As they approached the museum, a tank, out on exercises, rumbled thunderously across the road in front of the car. In the driving mirror, he saw Eric sit up and take notice.

'That's a Challenger,' he told him. 'Our main British battle tank. Crew of four – commander, gunner, loader, driver. One of the heaviest armoured and best protected tanks in the world.'

'It's got a great big gun in front.'

'High explosive squash head rounds,' the colonel continued, not bothering with any child-speak. 'Long range, very effective against buildings and thin-skinned vehicles. Gyrostabilized sight with laser rangefinder and night vision. The commander has eight periscopes to see all the way around in a circle and the turret can rotate in nine seconds.'

Eric had rotated himself to watch the tank rolling away over the snow.

'*Wow!*'

The colonel hadn't been in a tank regiment himself, but tanks were something pretty special in his view. And so were tank crews. He was well aware that the men that served in them were second to none.

In the museum, they walked around the halls, past the Shermans, the Matildas, the Panzers, the Crusaders and the Leopards. At each one, the colonel paused to give his grandson a brief account: number of crew, armaments, any interesting details – often quite lurid.

'The Germans called the Shermans "Tommy cookers".'

'Why?'

'Because they called British soldiers "Tommies" and when the Germans managed to hit one of the tanks, they often caught fire and sometimes the crew couldn't get out.'

'So they all got burned?'

'I'm afraid so, poor chaps.' They walked on. 'This is a German tank. A Panzer, also known as a Tiger. Lots of fire-power and armour but slow and too heavy to go over most bridges. It has a snorkel at the back so it can go through deep water. Crew of five.'

'Did they ever drown?'

'I expect so,' the colonel said briskly. 'Occasionally.'

Wherever there was something for children to push or pull, or listen to or wind-up, he pointed it out for Eric. They sat in a World War One trench and in a World War Two Anderson shelter. Eric went over an assault course, tried on an army helmet and had a go at the rifle range, shooting at targets and making a lot of noise. Then the colonel had a go with the Lee Enfield, too, and his score was pretty good. After that, they both tried the Bren Gun, *rat-a-tat-a-tat,* and then the PIAT.

'Projector, Infantry, Anti-Tank,' the colonel translated, not about to mince his words. 'Used in the Second World War. High explosive anti-tank projectile. Spring-loaded but only effective up to two hundred yards. Handy for close combat and urban warfare. Makes a hole in the tank and the frag-ments go everywhere. Not too good for the chaps inside it. Nowadays, the American A-10 Thunderbolt plane fires massive uranium armour-piercing shells from an Avenger Gatling gun. High muzzle velocity. Deadly accurate. Six direct hits and the tank's completely destroyed.'

They blew away the German tanks with the PIAT gun and the colonel's grandson beamed up at him. 'Mummy wouldn't let me do any of this. She'd say it was much too dangerous.'

'Then we won't tell her, will we?'

'No, we won't, Grandfather.'

The colonel looked down at the boy's flushed face and shining eyes and felt a sudden and quite unexpected bond of male solidarity. United they stood against the stupid fussing of women.

After two happy hours they went to the museum restaurant for lunch.

They ate fish and chips with bright green frozen peas and dollops of tomato ketchup, and afterwards, Eric had chocolate ice-cream. He also had two Fantas to drink.

'We won't tell Mummy about this either, Eric, will we?'

His grandson beamed at him again. 'No, we *won't*.'

Back at the cottage, the colonel unearthed the Clarks' shoebox that contained the old toy soldiers that he had played with as a child.

He and Eric lined them up in battle formations on the sitting room carpet and the colonel talked tactics and manoeuvres, outflanking and encirclement. Surprise attack, counter-attack, advance, retreat, capture and surrender. Later on, they had chicken nuggets with tinned baked beans and more chips, and then some more ice-cream – bright pink strawberry flavour this time.

At the end of a week, Marcus returned to collect Eric. Susan had been allowed home and the baby had been saved.

'By the way, they told me it's a girl,' Marcus whispered aside. 'But don't say anything to Susan, whatever you do. She wants it to be a surprise.'

The colonel stood at the cottage gate and waved as they drove off. He could see that his grandson had twisted around in his car seat and was waving happily to him through the back window.

Twelve

The snow was beginning to melt away quite fast. From her attic window, Jeanette could see patches of green appearing on the lawn and spreading.

The plate she was working on – a composition of willow warblers flying about – wasn't going very well. The shrubby background wasn't right and the birds looked as though they were stuffed. Furthermore, she was finding it hard to concentrate; her mind kept wandering and she kept getting up and walking around and staring out of the window.

The photo albums and the framed portraits were still hidden under her bed because Rex, the swine, seemed to have vanished into thin air. She had tried the London phone number he had given her and, after listening to his voice speaking on an answer machine, she had left a guarded message that said nothing except would he please get in touch. She'd tried twice more and left two more short, sharp messages and then given up. It was ironic that having spent the past months *not* wanting to see him at all, it was now urgent that she did.

Two days ago a removal van had arrived and Flat 2 had been cleared. She had watched the men carrying out Lois's furniture – the couches, the cushions, the tables, the lamps, the mirrors – all gone, lock, stock and barrel. The helicopter had not returned and Mrs Barnes had made no comment about any missing photos. If she had noticed, she probably thought that Bruce had taken them himself. Bruce himself would surely not be interested in them, except – as Rex had said – to throw them away. There was really nothing to worry about. Even so, she'd be relieved when they were out of her flat.

She had made a mug of coffee and settled down to work again when the flat bell rang suddenly, making her jump. Her heart was thumping as she went to open the door, but it was only the nice military man who had come to collect for the donkeys. The colonel who had found Lois.

He was very apologetic about disturbing her. He had tried to telephone first but been unable to find her number – no wonder since it was ex-directory, like Lois's. So, he had decided to walk over from his cottage on the green and Mrs Barnes had kindly let him in.

'I was wondering,' he went on, 'if you might be able to do a plate for me. A special commission.'

'I can certainly try.' She invited him to sit down. Studied him surreptitiously. He'd make a marvellous subject for a portrait: strong features, clear blue eyes, thick silver hair. Pretty old, of course, but still a handsome man. 'What sort of plate did you have in mind? Is it for someone particular, or for some occasion?'

'Both,' he said, with a smile. 'I have a second grandchild due to be born in May and I thought a plate might be a nice idea as a gift.'

'Do you happen to know if it's a boy or girl?'

'Girl.'

'Anything special in mind for her?'

He shook his head. 'Not really. I rather hoped you'd come up with some ideas.'

'Well . . .' she said slowly. 'With a new baby, it's often more a case of what would the parents like? It's really to please them. Fairies are very popular for little girls, of course. Small animals – field mice and hedgehogs and rabbits – all that sort of thing. And I did a very pretty plate for America recently, called "Gathering Violets" with a little girl picking wild violets in the spring. Flowers are always a safe bet.'

'How about not being quite so safe?'

She thought for a moment. 'I could do a kingfisher, perhaps. Have him swooping along a grassy river bank. Make it a May scene with a mass of bluebells in a wood behind. Not quite so pretty-pretty.'

'That's sounds very attractive.'

'I'll rough out some sketches for you. I expect you'll want her name and date of birth to go on it, won't you?'

He smiled. 'When I know them.' There was a pause. 'I have a grandson too, fifth birthday coming up soon. I wouldn't want him to feel left out of things.'

'Well, I could do one for him as well, if you like. What about an owl, or owls? Boys usually like those, especially if they're catching something. You know, a dead mouse hanging out of the beak, or skewered in the talons.'

'Actually, I was thinking of something rather different,' he said. 'I wondered if you could do a tank?'

She was taken aback. 'An army tank, you mean?'

'That's right. A British army tank: a Challenger.'

She'd seen squadron commemoration plates featuring old Second World War planes – Lancasters, Spitfires, Hurricanes . . . all that sort of thing – but never tanks. Machines of any kind were a very different matter. You had to understand how they worked and moved, and the engineering behind them, or they'd look as stuffed and soulless as the willow warblers.

'I'm not sure I could cope with that, Colonel.'

'I could let you have some photos and drawings if it would help.'

Truth to tell, she was getting awfully bored with pretty flowers and tweeting birds. 'Well, I'll give it a try . . . but I can't promise it'll be any good.'

'Thank you.'

As he was leaving, he said, 'Mrs Barnes told me that Miss Delaney's flat has been cleared out and that it's up for sale.'

'Yes. Bruce King didn't waste any time.'

'It's all been very sad, hasn't it? I remember you saying at the inquest what high spirits Miss Delaney was in when you saw her at Christmas.'

'That's right. She was very chuffed about the idea of working again.'

'You'd think that would have given her a good enough reason to live.'

'Yes, you would, wouldn't you? But she *was* a bit of a nut case.'

'You knew her rather well, I gather.'

'Yes, I did. And she often got very down – sometimes for no logical reason. Of course, the drink didn't help. It never really cheers people up, does it? Just makes them even more miserable.'

He nodded. 'That's quite true.'

She closed the door after him and went back to her trestle table and the willow warblers and picked up her paint brush again. A *tank*, for heaven's sake!

As the colonel reached the landing and was about to go down the main staircase, a door opened behind him. He turned to see Miss Quinn.

'Are you collecting for something again?'

'No, madam. I was calling on Miss Hayes.'

'They shouldn't let you in. Especially after what happened to that woman. The security's here's a disgrace.'

'You have nothing to fear from me and I am about to leave.'

She came closer and he looked at the thin, turned-down mouth, the sour expression. Poor woman, he thought, whatever happened to make her so bitter?

'I saw that girl go down to Flat Two that evening. She was ringing the doorbell.'

'Yes. Miss Hayes has confirmed that she did.'

'And there was another woman on the terrace, looking in windows, I said so to the police.'

'Whoever she was, they seem quite satisfied that she had nothing whatever to do with Miss Delaney's death.'

'How do they know that?'

'I expect they have their reasons.'

'I see everything that goes on here.'

He said politely, 'And I'm sure you were a great help to the police.'

'Mr King made a lot of noise when he arrived. He was angry about the front doorbell not working. I heard him swearing loudly. Disgusting language.'

'I'm sorry about that. Now, if you'll excuse me.' He turned to go down the stairs.

'When I saw him leaving after the news, I said to myself, Miss Delaney will be well rid of him. No wonder she wanted a divorce.'

The colonel's foot stopped on the third stair. He turned around.

'The news?'

'The BBC six o'clock news. I always watch it on my television.

'But you said *after* the news. You mean you saw him leaving when the six o'clock news had finished?'

'I just told you I did. I waited to see the weather forecast then I went to put the kettle on for a cup of tea, like I always do, and then I happened to take a look out on the landing, to make sure there was no more trouble going on. That's when I saw Mr King going.'

'Are you quite sure it was him?'

'Of course I am. I've got eyes in my head. I saw him open the front door and slip out. You can open it from the inside easily. It doesn't take a second.'

He stared up at her. Her eyes were glittering and he wondered if she was actually deranged.

'But you would only have seen his back, isn't that so? You wouldn't have seen his face.'

She glared. 'You're just like the police; you don't believe me. It was Mr King. He was wearing the same overcoat I'd seen when he came in. Expensive tweed. I suppose he hoped it would make him look like a country gentleman.'

'Did you go to the inquest on Miss Delaney's death, by any chance, Miss Quinn?'

'I've got better things to do with my time.'

'Mrs Barnes testified in court that Mr King left just after six. Her husband corroborates that. They both saw him out.'

'Well, they're both wrong. Or they're lying. He was alone and it was more like a quarter to seven.'

He walked on down the stairs. Miss Quinn was the one who must be lying. She and the Barnes's couldn't both be right and if he had to choose between them, he knew which version he'd go for.

In the hall, he hesitated uneasily for a moment. The matter needed some investigation but he could hardly go interrogating Mr and Mrs Barnes, like Inspector Squibb. He needed to think up an excuse for ringing at their door and bringing up the subject. After a while, one came to him.

He had a friend who was looking for a flat in a country house like the Hall, he told Mrs Barnes unblushingly when she opened her door. It was just possible that Flat 2 might suit him. Would it be possible to have a quick look so he could report back to him?

Mrs Barnes was willing to oblige, though, as she confessed to him when she unlocked the door, it still gave her the shivers to go in there.

She stood just inside the sitting-room doorway, waiting while he looked around. The room was completely bare, stripped of anything that had belonged to Lois Delaney – except for the now very faint scent of her French perfume. He went over to the French windows and peered out on to the terrace.

'My friend's quite concerned about security. He's away a lot – that's why he needs a place like this. Are the locks reliable?'

'Oh, yes, sir. Mr King insisted on the best quality.'

'How do these French windows work?'

'There's a key for the door handle and a separate one to undo the bolts at the top and bottom. You just push them up or down from the inside to make them lock again. The keys are kept on that hook there, by the door. Would you like me to show you, sir?'

'No, that won't be necessary, thank you, Mrs Barnes.'

She hesitated. 'They were all there on the hooks after Miss Delaney died, sir. And all the bolts in place. Nobody could have got in without breaking in, or gone out that way without leaving the door bolts undone behind them. You can only work those from the inside. That's what I've been thinking to myself.'

'Quite.' He'd been thinking the same thing. 'Are there

any security lights on the terrace– the kind that go on automatically if tripped?'

'Well, there used to be but Miss Delaney complained about them because they were so bright. We get a lot of foxes and badgers round here at night and they were always making the lights go on. She said it woke her up and frightened her. And Mr Avery in Flat One complained too. He said it was like living in a German POW camp. Just like Colditz, he said. The residents upstairs didn't care for them either. So, they were disconnected.'

'On Mr King's order?'

'It must have been. Or one of his people.'

He moved away from the windows. 'Well, I mustn't keep you, Mrs Barnes. I'm sure you're very busy.'

'There's always plenty to do, sir.'

He smiled at her. 'I hope you can sit down in the evenings and have some time to yourself.'

'I try to, sir.'

'I remember your mentioning that your husband always likes to watch the BBC six o'clock news.'

'That's quite right, sir. It's a real habit with him. I don't watch it myself. There's always too much bad news for my liking.'

'Didn't you say he had just started to watch it on New Year's Eve when Mr King came to complain about Miss Delaney's bell not working?'

'Yes. That's how we knew exactly what time he left. Stanley was sitting down, watching the headlines, when Mr King rang at our door and he had to get up again. Mr King gave him a real ticking-off and we were a bit worried he might give us the sack, truth to tell. He's always so particular about everything.'

'And your husband went on watching the news after Mr King had left?'

'That's right. He'd missed quite a lot, of course, by the time we'd seen Mr King out. Then, later on, around seven, Mr Avery came to the door with his Anglepoise lamp, wanting to know if Stanley could mend it. Like I said, there's always something needing doing.'

'I expect your husband's often asked to do odd jobs like that.'

'Oh, yes. He got the lamp going in a jiffy. It was only one of the wires loose. Nothing difficult.'

'Miss Delaney must have been very glad to have him around.'

'Yes, she was, sir. He was always helping her out.'

The colonel thanked Mrs Barnes for showing him the flat and promised to report to his imaginary friend. As she let him out of the front door, he noticed that it opened easily from the inside, without any sort of key or hidden tricks – just like Miss Quinn had told him.

'That Colonel bloke's been snooping about again. I can see him going off down the drive.'

'You're getting positively paranoid, Craig. Anyone would think you had a guilty conscience about something.'

'Well, what's he doing here?'

'Perhaps he came to view Flat Two. It might suit him.'

Craig shuddered. 'I don't know how anyone would want to live there – not after what happened. It's bad enough it's only next door to us.'

'My dear boy, people are always dying in houses and have done for hundreds of years. You mustn't be so squeamish.'

'Upstairs, though. In bed.'

'Not necessarily. They don't always go meekly up the stairs, lie down and die. They conk out all over the place – quite probably in this very room.'

Craig gave another shudder. It gave him the creeps, just thinking about it. She'd gone and topped herself in the bath. He wondered if they'd change it for the next person, or not bother.

He watched the bloke going out of the gate.

'Well, I wish that stupid woman had never come to live here. She's spoiled everything.'

'Nonsense. You're being dramatic, Craig, as well as paranoid. And Lois Delaney was far from stupid.'

'And I still don't see why you didn't tell me you knew her.'

'As I have already remarked on a number of occasions, I don't tell you everything about my past.'

Craig swung round from the window. 'Did you go and see her – that evening?'

'What evening?'

'New Year's Eve. When she snuffed it. You said you were going to see Mr Barnes about the lamp, but you took a bloody long time about it.'

Neville had stopped work, needle lifted in one hand, and he was staring at him.

'Why Craig, I do believe you suspect me of doing her in.'

He kicked at the carpet. 'Well, I think it's odd you took so long.'

'I was chatting to nice Mr Barnes.'

'What about?'

'That's none of your business, Craig. You really mustn't keep prying into every nook and cranny of my life. I simply won't allow it.'

He kicked at the carpet again. 'Sorry.'

'I'll forgive you, dear boy, but don't do it again. Now, take a look at this.'

Neville held up the latest Collector's Treasure – Queen Elizabeth the First complete with red wig, starched white lace ruff, gold stomacher and a red velvet gown sewn with a lot of sparkly, coloured glass jewels.

'Do come and give me your invaluable opinion on how this looks. I don't want to go over the top.' He smiled at Craig. 'You know me. I can get quite carried away.'

Inspector Squibb was no more appealing over the phone than in person.

'Good of you to call me, Colonel. The old girl did tell us about that.'

'She seemed very sure of her facts, Inspector. She says she saw Mr King leave *after* she'd finished watching the BBC six o'clock news. She insists that he left at about a quarter to seven.'

There was a faint sigh. 'I've come across a lot of people

like her in the course of my career, Colonel. Especially old women living alone. They like nothing better than to call attention to themselves. They make things up, if necessary. Anything to feel important, for once in their lives. Sometimes they really believe it; other times they just get muddled. Sometimes it's to get revenge as well as attention. And I dare say Miss Quinn's nose was out of joint at missing some of the action. After our investigations, I'm quite satisfied with everything that Mr and Mrs Barnes told us and they say they both saw Mr King leave the Hall just after six.'

'Well, I thought I should let you know about it, Inspector.'

'As I said, sir, I appreciate your calling me.'

The colonel put down the receiver. Duty had been done. Now surely he could forget all about the unhappy business of Lois Delaney. Put it out of his mind for ever. Miss Quinn had been mistaken or confused, to put a kind interpretation on it. If she had been watching the six o'clock news when Bruce King had actually left, she would not have seen him going. Like Stanley Barnes, the television evening news was probably a high point of Miss Quinn's day. The time when she sat glued to the screen, oblivious to all else, to focus vicariously on the world's disasters and miseries and scandals. Even on the weather forecast, for heaven's sake.

The fact was that Miss Quinn, the arch-snooper, was by no means infallible. She had spotted Jeanette Hayes ringing Lois Delaney's doorbell on New Year's Eve, but she missed seeing Roy Ward doing the same earlier. Nor had she seen Neville Avery taking his lamp to Mr Barnes for repair. And whoever she *had* seen going out of the front door couldn't have been Bruce King. If, indeed, it had been anybody at all.

Thirteen

The colonel had not bought any new shirts since before Laura had died. There hadn't seemed to be a great deal of point, and, in any case, the ones he already owned had been perfectly satisfactory until recently when he had begun to notice a frayed cuff here, a worn collar there. Time, perhaps, to make a trip to Jermyn Street where the January sales would be on. He'd make a day of it and stay the night at his club.

He phoned Alison to invite her to lunch.

'Not your gloomy old club, Dad,' his daughter told him. 'Let's go somewhere else.'

They arranged to meet at a restaurant he had heard of but never been to. One of the 'in' places.

The next day, he drove to Dorchester station, parked the car and caught the train to London. He took a taxi to his club, deposited his overnight case and went on to Jermyn Street where he bought four new shirts – expensive even in the sale, but undoubtedly worth it. He knew they would look good and wear well. For the hell of it, he also bought two new Italian silk ties – not in the sale.

He arrived early at the restaurant in Soho, before Alison, and waited for her at the bar just inside the entrance, people-watching with interest. The atmosphere was the opposite of the conventional decorum of his maligned club – full of buzz and action. It was obviously popular with the theatre crowd because he recognized several famous faces, one of which had been at Lois Delaney's funeral. This was, after all, in the middle of theatreland. The other customers were mostly young-ish and looked and sounded confident and highly successful, whatever their path or profession. They'd have to be, he thought drily, glancing at the prices on the menu he'd been given.

Alison arrived on time, dressed in her smart London clothes. Like her mother, though in a different way, she had style. As the song said, you'd either got it, or you hadn't got it. You couldn't buy style in a shop, or send for it from a mail-order catalogue; it was unbuyable and indefinable. His daughter's face lit up as she saw him and her smile reminded him for a second of the young Laura, her mother, and made him catch his breath.

'Hi, Dad! Great to see you. You're looking pretty good.'

'So are you, darling.'

They went through to the dining room and were shown to the table which Alison had pulled strings to get. The head waiter addressed her by name and his daughter was plainly on very familiar ground.

'The food's marvellous here, Dad. Nothing at all fancy, but they do it brilliantly. You can have things like sausages and mash, if you like, or shepherd's pie, or corned beef hash. The calf's liver's wonderful, so's the saddle of lamb and the Barbary duck's pretty good. I usually have the seared scallops.'

He chose the shepherd's pie. Naomi had once given him a simple recipe for the same dish but in his hands it had been a disaster. Cooks were born, not made, he reckoned; rather like gardeners. The wine he'd ordered arrived and they clinked glasses. Alison looked happy. He knew that she was extremely good at her job and had been made a director of her company, but he wished, in his old-fashioned way, that she would get married and settle down and have children. All she would ever say on the subject was that she had never met anyone she'd want to spend the rest of her life with, or who'd want to spend his with her. 'You and Mum are a hard act to follow,' was usually her comment. 'You set the bar pretty high.' It saddened him to think of her reaching his own age and still being alone. At least, he had the memories of his years of happiness with Laura to keep him company.

She asked him about Eric. 'How on earth did you manage to cope with that spoiled little horror, Dad?'

'I managed,' he said with a smile. 'He's not as bad as you think. As a matter of fact, we got on rather well in the end.'

'Good for you. I think I'd have strangled him if it had been me. And I'd probably strangle Susan, too, if I were Marcus. I hope she doesn't go and spoil the next one rotten when it finally arrives.'

There was no love lost between his daughter and his daughter-in-law – not so surprising when they were poles apart.

'How's that ratty old cat? Still with you?'

'Unfortunately.'

'Well, he's company – of a kind.'

'You make me sound like some old woman.'

'That's the last thing you'll ever be. But I wish you'd come back and live in London, Dad. You're miles away and it must be pretty lonely down there.'

She had wanted him to buy a flat in London – taken him to see several possibles – but he had decided against it. Alison had her own busy life to lead and he had no wish to intrude upon it. Also, London was an expensive place to live on an army pension and not much else.

Marcus and Susan had often tried to persuade him to live near them but he had resisted that, too – for different reasons. Susan would want to take him over. She'd want to come round daily with healthy casseroles and organic foodstuffs, and keep calling him Father, which he hated.

'London can be a very lonely place, too.'

'True. But there's such a lot going on here. You'd never get bored.'

'There's quite a lot going on in Frog End.'

His daughter pulled a face. 'Jumble sales and whist drives. Deadly lectures in the village hall.'

He said drily, 'Not to mention the Venture for Retired People.'

'The what?'

'Never mind. There's plenty to do, believe me.'

'Are you still treasurer of the summer fête?'

'I'm afraid so. It's practically a job for life.'

She pulled another face. 'After everything you did in the army, it seems a bit of a let down. You really ought to move back to civilization.' She leaned forward, lowering her voice. 'Hey, Dad, do you know that woman?'

'What woman?'

'The one two tables away on your left. She keeps looking at you.'

He glanced in that direction and encountered a steady gaze and a smile. Not young, but considerably younger than himself, and the smile was definitely come-hither. Or maybe he was imagining it? If he wasn't careful, he'd end up like Major Cuthbertson, convinced that every attractive woman was lusting after him.

'No, I don't know her.'

Alison said, amused, 'Well, she fancies you, Dad. You're still a very good-looking bloke, you know. Still knock 'em in the aisles. No chance you've met anyone else, I suppose? Marcus and I would be thrilled – so long as she was good enough for you and you'd be happy.'

He *had* met someone, as it happened, and he had become obsessed by her – but not in the way that Alison meant. A dead woman whom he had never known when she was alive but who he could not get out of his mind.

'No, I'm afraid not.'

'Oh, well, we live in hope. It's bound to happen – sooner or later.'

The shepherd's pie arrived, together with the scallops, and it was as good as Alison had promised. Even better, in fact.

She said suddenly, 'I read all about Lois Delaney's suicide in the papers, Dad. Couldn't believe she was living in Frog End. I wouldn't have thought it was her sort of place at all.'

'It was only temporary.'

'Did you ever meet her there?'

'Not exactly.'

'What do you mean, not exactly?'

He explained.

She stared at him in astonishment. '*You* were the one

who found her? You didn't tell me about that. How on earth did that happen?'

He explained a bit more. No point telling her about his ridiculous conviction that the corpse of Lois Delaney had wanted to speak to him, and that she had not committed suicide at all. Alison would think he had started to go senile. 'I just happened to be there. Pure chance.'

'Good heavens! It must have been horrible.'

'It was certainly very sad.'

'Funnily enough, I met her agent, Magda Dormon, before Christmas – at a publicity do. Quite a character. She dresses like a man and acts like one. She started talking to me about Lois Delaney and saying she was going to make a big come-back. It's the sort of thing all theatrical agents say, of course. So-and-so's going to hit the big time, be a big star, go to Hollywood, make a big comeback. It's part of their job. I didn't believe a word of it, really. Lois Delaney was long past it, wasn't she? She must have been seventy at least.'

'She was exactly my age, as it happens,' he said drily.

'Sorry, Dad. But you know what I mean. There aren't many good parts for women once they pass the thirty-five mark. Let alone later.'

Rex Farrell had called Lois Delaney's agent a fearful old dyke, but he had also said that she had been very loyal and done her best. To the end, it seemed.

He said, 'Is she a well-known agent?'

'Magda Dormon? Yes, she is, though she's getting a bit past it, too. I've seen her in here once or twice. I think her office is somewhere nearby.'

They had chocolate soufflé afterwards and then coffee. Alison looked at her watch.

'Lord, is that the time! I'm really sorry, Dad, but I've got to fly. I've got a meeting at two thirty. Don't you move, they'll get me a taxi. Thanks so much for the lunch.'

She kissed him and rushed off and he finished his coffee and paid the bill. When he left the room, the woman at the nearby table smiled up at him as he passed. He smiled back. No, he hadn't imagined it.

He collected his coat and the Jermyn Street carrier bag

from the cloakroom and asked the girl in charge if she knew where Magda Dormon worked.

'I'm afraid I don't, sir.'

The doorman was better informed. 'Miss Dormon? She's a regular customer here, sir. Her office is on Shelton Street. Just around the corner. I believe it's a few doors down on the left.'

He walked slowly along the street, peering at doorways until he saw the brass sign that he was looking for – small and in need of a polish: *Magda Dormon. Theatrical Agent.*

Inside, the building was dark and dingy, the staircase uncarpeted, the paint flaking. Somehow he would have expected Lois Delaney's agent to work from somewhere much better, but then he knew nothing about the theatrical world. Perhaps agents were judged by their results, not by their surroundings. At the top of the stairs he found a door with another sign – painted on wood this time. When he knocked, there was an answer from within that sounded like a harsh croak. He opened the door cautiously.

A small, squat person was sitting on the other side of a desk, dressed, as Alison had described, in men's clothing – dark suit and waistcoat, white shirt, red and white spotted bow tie. The hair was cut short and dyed bright orange, the head broad, the nose flat, the mouth wide and rubber-lipped, the eyes bulbous. He was reminded of a frog – an exotic, brightly-coloured foreign variety, a very distant cousin to the humble green ones that lived in his pond at the cottage. He would not have been surprised if the nicotined fingers that held a cigarette had been webbed.

'Miss Dormon?'

Another harsh croak. 'Yes? What do you want?'

The ashtray on the desk was full of squashed stubs, the air thick with stale smoke. The colonel had smoked plenty in his time before he had given up, but he'd forgotten how disagreeable the habit could be.

He introduced himself. 'I've come about the late Lois Delaney.'

'What about her?'

'I believe you were her agent?'

'For more than thirty years. She never mentioned you.'

'No, she wouldn't have done. We never actually met.'

'So, what are you doing here?'

He explained as best he could. She looked unimpressed.

'You still haven't told me why you're here.'

'Frankly, I'm puzzled by her suicide. I understand that she'd been offered a leading role in a Noël Coward revival in the West End?'

'That's right. Judith Bliss in *Hay Fever*. Damn good play and she'd have been a big hit.'

'Her husband, Mr King, testified at the inquest into her death that she'd asked him to put up money for it.'

'Can't think why she'd bother to do that. There were already enough backers in the bag.'

'Mr King said Miss Delaney didn't trust them not to pull out.'

'Codswallop! It was all fixed. I told her so. She'd no need to ask him for a brass farthing. Besides, she knew the score with Bruce. It would have been a waste of breath. He lost a packet once before backing a play she was in and raised merry hell. Can't blame him, really. Anyway, they were getting divorced, so he wasn't going to feel any obligation, was he?'

'I imagine not.'

'Of course, she might have asked him just for the hell of it. To get up his nose and make him look a mean bastard – which he was. I wouldn't have put that past her.'

'Was she looking forward to returning to the West End?'

'What do you think, Colonel? She'd been out in the cold for years. When I phoned her about it, she was thrilled to bits. Over the moon. It was a wonderful chance for her and, like I said, she'd have been a big hit. Lord knows why she went and killed herself, the silly goose, but then she was always unpredictable. Up and down, all the time. Maybe she got cold feet. Maybe she decided she couldn't cope after so long away from the theatre. She used to suffer from bad stage fright in the early days and it never really goes, you know. Maybe she was afraid of failure and bad notices from the critics. They can be crucifying unless you've got a hide like a rhinoceros, and she hadn't.' A long, choking drag on the cigarette, a sideways look from the bulging frog's eyes. 'Actors are like children, Colonel. They need their hands held a lot. Someone to keep telling them how wonderful they are. I did my best with Lois but I couldn't be there all the time.'

'I'm sure you did everything possible, Miss Dormon.'

'I just wish she hadn't done it. It would have been good to see her back again. She was a class act. A real star, and there aren't many of them left.'

The croak had softened and he realized that Magda Dormon's regret for her late client was genuine – not just for the lost percentage.

'Yes, it's a great shame.'

'Nothing to be done about it, Colonel. She's gone and there's an end to it. The show must go on.'

He offered his sympathy and left.

He walked down Charing Cross Road and went into Foyle's bookshop to browse through the military history section. His mind, however, kept wandering back to Lois Delaney. Damn it, why couldn't he forget all about her? Why did thoughts keep nagging at him?

Magda Dormon had not understood why Lois would have bothered to ask her soon-to-be-ex husband to back the play, but the agent had not seemed very surprised at Lois Delaney's suicide, given her unstable temperament, her volatile moods and the fact that she had suffered badly from stage fright. The twin sister had not been surprised either for much the same reasons, except that she had not mentioned the stage fright because she had probably not known about it. After all, she had seen very little of her sister once they had grown up. It was their old nanny who had been close to Lois Delaney: the one whom she visited regularly in Caister-on-Sea; the one to whom she told everything and who always understood. Nanny Oliver.

There were more than twenty residential homes for the elderly in Caister-on-Sea and the colonel had walked the bleak sea front and the windy side streets to call at seven of them before he struck lucky.

'Miss Oliver's in the conservatory,' he was told by an aproned woman. 'She always sits there. I'll point her out to you.'

The central heating was overpowering, and there was a smell of past meals and disinfectant. In the lounge, he passed a row of old ladies propped like rag dolls in chairs in front of a television set that was showing a cooking programme. Some young chef was busy making a cheese soufflé, brandishing whisks and graters. It seemed unlikely that any of the viewers present would ever do so much as boil an egg again. There were no old gentlemen among the ladies, which was to be expected. Wives usually outlived their husbands – except in his case. Perhaps, though, it was a blessing in disguise for the men – not to be ending their days like this.

Nanny Oliver was sitting alone in a wheelchair in the conservatory. It was a bright and pleasant room and not so over-heated as the rest of the home. There were some potted palms and a view over a garden which had a few good trees, some dull-looking shrubs and an expanse of rather patchy lawn. The bird table, sited immediately outside the windows, was occupied by a grey squirrel gnawing a crust of bread held in its front paws.

Nanny Oliver had been reading a book and she raised her head slowly at his approach. There was a plaid rug tucked round her legs and one side of her body bore evidence of the stroke that Iris Delaney had spoken of – the left foot resting at an awkward angle, the arm lying uselessly in her lap, the affected face muscles. But the colonel could tell by the look in her eyes, that though her body might have let her down, her mind was still perfectly agile.

He sat down in a chair beside her and, once more, he found himself explaining his intrusion on a stranger. She was not, he realized instinctively, the sort of person who would take kindly to half-truths or prevarication and so he gave it to her straight. The whole story. While he was talking, she studied him over the spectacles on the end of her nose and he found himself hoping that his tie was straight and that his fingernails were clean. When he had finished, she asked more or less the same question as Magda Dormon.

'Why should you care about Lois?'

He said, 'I'm not quite sure. At the inquest, the coroner was satisfied that she had taken her own life. There was certainly plenty of evidence that she was subject to mood swings and depression. Is that so in your experience?'

'Oh, yes. Since she was a little girl. I always used to tell her that she was like the Grand Old Duke of York. When she was up, she was up; and when she was down, she was down.' The speech was slow, but perfectly clear. 'It's quite probable that she killed herself. She told me that she often felt like doing that.'

'Her twin sister, Iris, says that you knew her better than anyone and that she always confided in you. I wondered what she had told you on the last occasion when you saw her.'

She plucked at the plaid rug. 'What do you want to know exactly, Colonel?'

'Well, Mr King testified in court that Miss Delaney had written to him asking him to call at her flat. When he did so on New Year's Eve, she asked him for money to back the Noël Coward play. She became hysterical when he refused. Do you think that's possible, too?'

'It's possible, but I don't think she needed to ask him for any money. I understood that the funding had all been arranged. That's what she told me.'

'Her agent told me the same. But Mr King maintained that she was afraid of the backers withdrawing. It had happened to her before, apparently.'

'That's possible, too. I can only tell you that when Lois came to see me just before Christmas, I hadn't seen her so happy for years. Everything was suddenly going right for her, she said. She'd be back in the West End and she'd soon be divorced and free of Bruce King. And she'd never have to worry about money again.'

He smiled faintly. 'Not with a divorce settlement of twenty million pounds – so I heard.'

'Twenty? Not twenty. More than that. *Much* more.'

'Oh? How much more?'

'Fifty million pounds. Lois said that her lawyer was insisting on it, and not a penny less.'

'That's a very large sum.'

'I agree with you, Colonel. But Lois told me her husband was worth more than three hundred million and so he could easily afford it. Her lawyer was used to handling the big divorces and he knew exactly how to get her what she was entitled to. The judge would agree because her husband had used her as a business asset for nearly ten years. She'd been a great help to him and his company and now he was going to have to pay for it. That's what she told me. And she said that Bruce would hate parting with so much money, especially since he'd know that Rex would get most of it in the end. He'd hate that more than anything, she said, and it amused her. Made her laugh. I told her that she was asking for trouble. Playing with fire.'

'You looked after her son when he was small, didn't you? What do you think of him?'

'Rex is like his mother. Too handsome and too charming for his own good. And he's very lazy – which Lois wasn't. But he's a kind person at heart. He comes to see me too – not very often, but he comes. A good boy, really.'

The squirrel had polished off the bread and was scampering away.

The colonel got to his feet. 'Well, I mustn't keep you, Miss Oliver.'

'There's nothing to keep me from.' She looked up at him. 'I told Lois not to imagine that all that money would bring her happiness because it wouldn't. No matter how many millions. Or Rex, either. I warned her. It never does, does it?'

'No,' he agreed. 'It doesn't seem to.'

She sighed. 'I haven't been much help, I'm afraid, Colonel. I haven't the strength any more to be of use to anybody. You must do what you think is right. Whatever you feel is necessary.'

The cookery programme had changed to a different one about doing up a Spanish villa. A blonde and smiling girl in very short shorts was whitewashing an outside wall in bright sunshine and talking about how easy it would be to install a jacuzzi. The old ladies had all dropped off to sleep, chins on their chests.

On the train journey back to London, the colonel stared out of the window at the winter landscape and thought about what he'd learned and about what might have happened on that snowy New Year's Eve, and about what Lois Delaney's silenced mouth might have been trying to say.

Fourteen

The offices of the BHK Group were located on the top floors of a soaring steel and glass tower on the north bank of the Thames. Surveying its dizzy heights from ground level, the colonel thought it was undeniably impressive – a magnificent counting house where the King could count out his money.

The entrance was closely guarded. However, the guardian happened to be an ex-sergeant major from his own regiment, which worked like a magic password. He went in, found the elevators and took one of them up to the top floor. The receptionist there was as steely as her surroundings.

'I'm afraid you won't be able to see Mr King without an appointment, sir. His diary is fully booked.'

He said pleasantly, 'This is a personal matter, not business. I think he'll see me, if you give him my name and say that it's in connection with his late wife.'

'He's in a meeting at the moment.'

'Then I'll wait.'

He sat on a very comfortable and expensive white leather sofa and picked up a copy of *The Financial Times*. People came and went around him and after half an hour or so, the receptionist came over.

'Mr King says he's too busy to see you, sir. Perhaps you would care to make a future appointment?'

He smiled at her. 'No, thank you. I'll wait until he's free today. I've got plenty of time.'

He finished reading *The Financial Times* and turned to the crossword.

He was halfway through it when another woman came over, perfectly groomed and also made of steel.

'I'm Mr King's secretary. He says he can give you ten minutes, Colonel. If you'd care to come this way.'

He followed her and she conducted him into a very large room.

You couldn't, he thought, exactly call it an office. There was no desk of any kind – just more white leather sofas, black glass tables, outsize modern art canvases on the walls, concealed spot lighting and what seemed like acres of white-tiled floor. The view through the floor-to-ceiling windows was breathtaking. The Thames lay far below, snaking its way into the hazy distance, and London was spread out gloriously before him.

'You've got precisely ten minutes, Colonel.' Bruce King had entered suddenly, like some pantomime demon king. He glanced at his watch. 'That's all I can spare you.'

'Yes, your secretary told me.'

'So, what's this about?'

'It concerns your wife, Lois Delaney.'

'My wife passed away earlier this month.'

'I know. I found her body.'

The tycoon frowned. 'Oh, yes, I remember you now. You were at the inquest. Well, what's your problem?'

'I don't think she killed herself, Mr King. That's my problem.'

The frown deepened to irritation. 'Don't waste my time. You heard the verdict. It wasn't an accident.'

'No, indeed it wasn't. You killed her.'

They were standing facing each other. Being several inches the taller gave the colonel a certain advantage because the other man was forced to look up to him.

Bruce King exploded. 'You've got a bloody nerve, I must say – insinuating your way in here to tell me some rubbish like that. Are you mad? Get out!'

The colonel stayed. 'I know how you did it. And why you did it.'

'*Really?*' The sarcasm was biting. 'I suppose it's money you're after? Is this a clumsy attempt at some kind of black-mail? If so, I'm calling the police immediately.'

'It's not blackmail, Mr King. I'm not interested in any money.'

'Everyone is, Colonel. There are no exceptions.'

'I'm one.'

'Then you're the first I've ever met. So, you think I killed my wife? Just how do you suppose I managed to do that? You were at the inquest. You heard the evidence. I'd left the house. I was on my way back to London.' He glanced again at his watch. 'You have eight more minutes.'

'You'd left the house, yes. And you were seen to drive off. But you returned. Your wife hadn't asked you to call on her, Mr King, nor did she ask you to put up any money to back the play. You went to see her because you had discovered that her lawyer was asking for a fifty million-pound settlement and you had been told that she was very likely to get it. You don't part with money easily – not after a lifetime's hard work – and certainly not such a huge amount. And there was also the matter of her son, Rex. You knew that your wife would keep on giving him hand-outs and that he would inherit the lot when she died. Your lazy, good-for-nothing, freeloading stepson whom your wife adored but whom you loathed and despised.'

'That's the first true thing you've said so far, Colonel. Seven minutes to go.'

'Your own son died as a child – the beloved boy who should have been your heir. The prospect of Rex Farrell cleaning up instead was intolerable. Unbearable. You had been prepared to go along with a twenty million court settlement for your wife, but fifty million was too much. Too large a slice of the cake that it had taken so long to bake. The only way to stop that happening was to kill her *before* the divorce was finalized and make it seem like suicide.'

'And how exactly did I manage that? With smoke and mirrors?'

'It was simple. When you called at the Hall on New Year's Eve you made certain that the Barnes's knew exactly when you arrived and exactly what time you left by pretending that the outside bell was faulty. Your wife was in a very happy and conciliatory mood and she told you about her chance of returning to the West End. You suggested a drink to toast the good news – a Bloody Mary which you knew she always kept ready-mixed in the fridge. As soon as she went into the kitchen to fetch it, you put your gloves on again and unlocked and unbolted the French windows behind the curtains. You knew exactly where the keys were kept and how the locks worked. Mrs Barnes told me that you had supervised everything done to the house. You pride yourself on being personally involved in every detail.'

'You're damn right I do. That's how I make my money, Colonel.'

'So, if your wife had come back into the room too soon, you would simply have told her that you were checking on the security locks. You had originally planned to tell the police that she had been very depressed when you saw her, and so the news of her comeback was a problem. Instead, you invented the story of her being frightened that the backers would pull out and begging you for the money.'

'Four minutes left, Colonel.'

'After the Barnes's had gone with you to the front door, you drove away from the Hall but stopped further along the road. There was a risk of your car being noticed but Frog End isn't known for its night revellers, even on a New Year's Eve, and you weren't going to be long. You walked back, cutting across the lawn to the terrace where you knew the security lights were out of action. There was no need to worry about making tracks because it was snowing heavily and the weather forecast had predicted that it would go on for most of the night. Your tracks would be well covered. Once again, you wore your gloves to avoid leaving finger-prints anywhere that might incriminate you.

'You had been married to your wife for nearly ten years, Mr King. You knew all about her habit of taking an early bath in the evenings, and that she always kept a hairdryer on her dressing table. You let yourself in through the French windows then locked and bolted them behind you. Your shoes would have had snow on them, of course, and you took those off so as not to leave any marks in the bedroom.

'Your wife was already in the bath, the door slightly ajar.

It only needed seconds to fetch the hairdryer, plug it into the socket by the door, switch it on and then throw it into the bath. It was very quick and easy. You took another risk when you left the house by the front door, but there was no alternative – the French windows had to be left locked and bolted inside, the keys on the hook. In fact, you've been taking calculated risks for most of your life. You thrive on them.'

'That's the second true thing you've said.'

The colonel paused. He said quietly, 'Only I think that in that very last moment she saw you, didn't she? She caught sight of you through the part-open door and she saw what you were going to do. She started to speak before she died. The only thing Lois Delaney begged of you that evening, Mr King, was not for you to back her play, but to spare her life.'

They faced each other across the white-tiled floor. It was a stand-off, as in Wild West films, the colonel thought, except that neither of them carried a gun to draw fast from the hip.

He went on, 'As a matter of fact, you *were* seen when you left the flat for the second time, later that evening. Seen in the hall, letting yourself out of the front door at a quarter to seven.'

Bruce King shrugged. 'The police told me a crazy old woman had told them some such story. They didn't believe a word of it. I was on my way back to London then. My wife died by her own hand, not mine, Colonel. She was very unstable – everyone knew that. Completely unbalanced. The big comeback would never have worked. But, as it happens, I worshipped her. It was *she* who wanted the divorce, not me. I never wanted our marriage to end. And you'd never be able to prove your ridiculous theory, Colonel. Your word against mine. Not much of a contest, I'd say.' Another glance at the watch. 'Your time's up.'

There was a clicking sound from a machine on one of the tables. The secretary's clipped voice spoke. 'Your next meeting is due to start, Mr King.'

Bruce King went over and flicked a switch. 'My visitor is just leaving.'

The ex-sergeant major hailed a taxi for him. As it sped along the Thames embankment, the colonel reflected that it was entirely possible that Bruce King had loved his wife – in his fashion – while she had tired of him, in the same way as she had tired of her previous husbands. Like goddesses, women such as Lois Delaney were more prudently worshipped from afar.

Fifteen

Freda Butler, watching from her sitting-room window, saw the colonel's Riley motor car travelling smoothly along the road around the village green. A moment or two earlier, the Cuthbertsons' Escort had gone by. She had known it was Mrs Cuthbertson driving, not the major, by the way the car had bounced along like a kangaroo and by the way it had veered so sharply into the driveway of Shangri-La, narrowly missing the gate post. Mrs Cuthbertson would have been returning from one of her ladies' bridge afternoons. Miss Butler would have liked to take part in them, but bridge had never been her game. Her late father, who had been an excellent player, had tried to teach her once but had soon lost patience.

A while before Mrs Cuthbertson had driven past, Miss Butler had observed Dr Harvey's grey Renault emerging from the Manor gateway and her hopes had been raised. So far as she knew, Ruth was in perfect health and so it was likely to have been a purely social call – unless, of course, the doctor was particularly interested in plants. She rather thought, though, that he was much more interested in Ruth.

She consulted her wristwatch. The afternoon train from London must have been late, which was not unusual – unless the colonel had stopped in Dorchester to do some shopping. It was known that he had gone to stay overnight in London because Mrs Dibbs had seen him waiting on the London platform with a small suitcase as she had arrived from Weymouth.

He had stayed at his club, no doubt. Gentlemen were very fortunate to have their clubs. Her father had spent a great deal of time in his after his retirement. Ladies were only permitted to enter a separate annexe, but, in any case, he had never invited her there.

The colonel's car had stopped outside the church lychgate and she could see that he was getting out, carrying something. Miss Butler hurried to fetch the U-boat commander's binoculars and trained them on the colonel. It was a bouquet of flowers – pure white lilies, which must have been quite expensive. She tracked her quarry through the lychgate until he was lost to view around the east side of the church. Miss Butler lowered the binoculars, puzzled. The colonel was a relative newcomer to Frog End and had never mentioned knowing any of the occupants of the graveyard. The expensive lilies would surely not have been intended for old Mrs Tanner who had been buried last month and had not been in her right mind for many years. Then her brow cleared. The only possibility was that the colonel was taking them to Miss Delaney's grave. Some kind of belated tribute? The gallant and respectful gesture of a gentleman who had had the misfortune to be unwittingly involved in her passing? She waited and, after a while, the colonel reappeared and got back into his car to drive on to his cottage.

The Save the Donkey collection had been very satisfactory: the total amount the highest ever. Miss Butler wondered if she could prevail on the dear colonel to help with the Red Cross collection coming up in May. He was so reliable – quite unlike Major Cuthbertson.

She swept the green once more with the binoculars. The snow was melting fast – larger and larger areas of muddy grass reappearing. Soon, it would all be gone and she would not be sorry to see January go as well. One way and another, it had not been a good month. February had the advantage of being short and it meant that winter was coming to an end at last. She liked to think of the year as clock-shaped with December at twelve o'clock and the other months spaced out accordingly. Once you got to two o'clock, spring was only just around the corner.

Thursday did not appear to have stirred from his place on the sofa but his food bowl was empty, licked clean, and he appeared in the kitchen when the colonel was refilling it. The usual critical sniffing went on, but less protracted than usual and he left the cat to a chopped chicken and liver feast and went upstairs to unpack his overnight case. That done, he went downstairs to the sitting room where he lit the fire, drew the curtains and sat in the wing chair for a while with his thoughts. He had let Lois Delaney down. Like Magda Dormon, he had done his best, and, like the agent, his best had not proved to be adequate. The lilies had been a kind of propitiation for his failure. He had laid them on her grave with his regrets and apologies.

There was no chance of proving anything against Bruce King because there was no proof. His theory remained, in the tycoon's very accurate words, only a theory. And possibly a ridiculous theory. It could have been a product of his imagination, springing from some unbalanced reaction to the discovery of the actress's body. Lois Delaney had, as her sister had shrewdly observed, exerted a powerful fascination on people and she had done so on him. Even after death. He had been a moth still drawn inexorably to an extinguished flame. Or, to put it less poetically, a mesmerized old fool.

He put on his *Mikado* record and listened to Yum-Yum singing her beautiful solo in the beginning of the second act. It stopped him thinking about Lois Delaney and he thought, instead, of Laura. The *Mikado* had been her favourite Gilbert and Sullivan and she had loved this particular song.

> *The sun, whose rays*
> *Are all ablaze*
> *With ever-living glory,*
> *Does not deny*
> *His majesty –*
> *He scorns to tell a story!*
> *He don't exclaim,*
> *'I blush for shame,*
> *So kindly be indulgent.'*

A loud banging at the door broke the magic spell and brought him back to reality; he went to open the front door to Naomi. The fur hat had been replaced by what seemed to be a lumberjack's tartan cap with ear-flaps, and the red cape by a long waxed cotton coat which reached to her ankles and her white trainers. The coat had a large collar, many pockets, a long brass zip and several leather straps secured by buckles. They both struggled for some minutes to remove it.

'Damned Australian thing,' she said, stepping out over one of the still-fastened straps and revealing her purple tracksuit, like a colourful insect emerging from its dull cocoon. 'The daughter-in-law brought it over as a Christmas present. Apparently, the Aussies wear them when they're riding around in the Outback during what they call "The Wet". I haven't ridden a horse in years and I've no intention of doing so again, so it's not much use to me.'

'Is the cap Australian, too?'

'No, Canadian,' she said, dragging it off. Underneath, her grey thatch stuck up like a scrubbing brush. 'I found it in the same trunk as the wolf-fur hat. My grandfather did a stint in the Rockies when he was young. Hideous thing, really, but it keeps the ears warm.'

The colonel hung the colonial garments up on the coat stand and led the way into the sitting room. Yum-Yum's solo had finished and she was singing happily with Pitti-Sing, Nanki-Poo and Pish-Tush about her wedding day. He turned off the record. Thursday was summarily dislodged as Naomi claimed the fire end of the sofa and rubbed her hands at the blaze.

'Good trip to London, Hugh?'

He sat down in the wing-back chair. 'How on earth did you know I'd gone there?'

'You can't go anywhere without most people in the village knowing about it. Especially not to London. The platform is under constant surveillance by our local KGB. How was it?'

'Good in parts, like the curate's egg. I had lunch with my daughter and I bought some new shirts in the Jermyn Street sales. And I also bought two ties – not in the sales.'

'What about the bad parts?'

'We don't talk about those.'

She nodded. 'Fair enough. Anyway, I've got something really good to tell you. I went round to the Manor this morning – to give Ruth a hand – and guess what I saw in one of the greenhouses?'

'I've no idea. Some special plant flowering?'

'No. Nothing to do with plants.' Naomi was looking positively triumphant. 'Try again.'

'A rare butterfly?'

'Wrong.'

'A hedgehog?'

'Wrong again.'

'Then I give up.'

She slapped her purple knee hard with one hand. 'I saw Ruth and Tom Harvey in a clinch.'

He smiled broadly. 'That's a very old-fashioned word.'

'I'm an old-fashioned person. Luckily, they didn't see me and I scarpered PDQ. What do you think about that?'

'It sounds promising.'

'It can only mean one thing, in my view. Neither's the type to play fast and loose.'

'Clinch? Fast and loose?' The colonel chuckled. 'Not many young people today would have the faintest idea what you're talking about, Naomi.'

'Well, *you* know perfectly well, don't you?'

'Yes, and I hope you're right.'

'Just think, Hugh. A wedding in Frog End, instead of a funeral. Wouldn't that be nice?'

The grandfather clock, tick-tocking away quietly in its corner, struck six with quick, silvery chimes. Naomi pricked up her ears like Pavlov's dog and the colonel rose dutifully to his feet.

'Time for a whisky. Will you have one?'

He was already moving towards the decanter tray, without waiting for her answer since he knew it well. She took the Chivas Regal – a good three-finger slug with just a splash of water, no ice – and raised the glass to him.

'Let's drink to them, Hugh. To Ruth and Tom.'

'I'll second that,' he said.

When she opened the door, he was standing there and smiling his quirky smile. He was wearing a foreign-looking overcoat that had probably cost a small fortune, the collar turned up around his ears, hands thrust deep in his pockets – rather like the famous photo of James Dean walking through New York.

She said coldly, 'I've been trying to get hold of you for ages, Rex.'

'I know. I heard the messages. Sorry, I've been in Prague, shooting that TV series. Bloody exhausting it was, too. I only got back today. Drove straight down hot foot to see you.'

'You'd better come in.'

He strolled into the flat and went over towards the trestle table where she had been sitting. 'Busy with the plates?'

'Don't sneer. They pay.'

'I'm not sneering.' He bent over the table. 'Hallo, what's this one? I thought you always did birds and flowers?'

'It's a tank.'

'I can see that. Bit of a departure for you, isn't it, Jeanie?'

'A retired colonel commissioned it for his grandson.'

'Not the one who found Mama?'

'Yes, as a matter of fact.'

'I liked him. Typical old soldier. Just the man to have beside you in a tight spot. A dying breed, I fear.' Rex bent lower, examining the plate. 'This is *very* good, Jeanie. You should do more of them. What kind of tank is it?'

'A Challenger. The British Army's latest.'

'I'm amazed we've still got any. I thought they'd all been scrapped. How did you get it so accurate?'

'The colonel lent me books and drawings. It wasn't too difficult. How was Prague?'

'Bloody cold. It's been snowing there, as well. Nice old city, though. Bags of atmosphere. Rather like Vienna. Very *Third Man*. Thank God we didn't have to go splashing about in the sewers.'

'Did the filming go all right?'

'The director seemed to think so. He thinks it's going to be a big success. That I'll wow the housewives with my mean and moody cop.'

'I hope you do.'

'Thank you, Jeanie. It's nice to know you care. It means a lot to me.'

He had turned round to look at her – slowly and deliberately – and she clenched her fists. Don't let him work the old charm. Don't fall for it. Not any more.

'I got the photographs for you, Rex.'

'I gathered as much from your cryptic messages. I'm very grateful. You're an angel.'

'I'll go and get them.'

She went to the bedroom, came back with the black bin liner and handed it to him. She watched while he took out the studio portraits and the six albums and placed them on the table.

'I left a few of the framed pictures behind, Rex. Someone was bound to notice if they all disappeared.'

'Smart thinking.' He was turning the leaves of one of the albums. 'Talk about a trip down Memory Lane. It's wonderful to have these. Bless you for it.'

She said, 'Your mother was very lovely.'

'Yes, she was, wasn't she? Right to the end. Life isn't going to be at all the same without her.'

He had said it casually, but she knew that he really meant it. She could hear it in his voice. 'You weren't a bad-looking child either.'

'I was much too pleased with myself. Still am.' He smiled at her. 'As you well know, Jeanie. You know all my sins, don't you?'

He was incorrigible, she thought, knees weakening. The TV series might, or might not, be a success. And even if it was, he might get bored with it or find it all too much like hard work. Too exhausting, like it had been in Prague.

'Well, you'd better be getting back to London.'

'I hoped you might offer me supper.'

'I haven't got anything except eggs.'

'That suits me fine. You could make those fluffy omelettes you always did so well. The ones where you whip up the whites first. I always used to love them.'

'If you promise to leave straight away afterwards.'

He held up his hand stiffly, thumb bent across like a boy scout. 'I swear I will.'

He wouldn't, of course. They'd open a bottle of wine and he'd make some excuse about being over the limit. And, God help her, she'd probably be fool enough to let him stay.

'What's the matter *this* time, Craig?'

'Nothing.'

'There very obviously is. You've been brooding away in that chair for the best part of an hour. You're not still thinking about Lois Delaney, are you? Imagining that I killed her off – *en passant,* as it were? Popped in and out of her flat and did the deed in a flash?'

''Course not.'

'I swear to you that I did nothing of the sort. I'm the mildest of creatures. I wouldn't harm a fly. You know that perfectly well.'

He did know it and he felt ashamed of what he'd been thinking. It seemed silly now. 'It's the weather,' he said. 'It's been getting me down. We're stuck in here day after day and I'm fed up with it.'

'You've got the January blues, dear boy. That's all.'

'It's more than that. I'm getting sick of the bloody country.'

'Now, now. This is a very nice place to be.'

'There's nothing to do and nowhere to go. It's fucking dreary.'

He didn't usually swear much because Neville didn't like it, but he was that pissed off.

'Well, you could give me a hand with my next project – perhaps that would help. I need ideas. Queen Elizabeth the First is all complete. Who shall I do next? You choose.'

He couldn't think of a thing. 'Don't know.'

'Come on, Craig. Use your brain and come up with something really good. Another historical figure, perhaps?'

He remembered history lessons at school. The teacher couldn't keep order and nobody'd paid much attention. He'd only listened if there was anything interesting. He'd quite liked the Tudors. Henry VIII and all those wives – the randy old sod – and chopping off people's heads whenever he felt like it. The lessons had got boring after he'd died, what with the weedy son next and then that grim old cow, Mary. But after her, Queen Elizabeth had livened things up, seeing off the Spics and everything. Nobody'd got the better of *her*. Took after her dad – red hair, temper and all. She didn't take any bloody crap from anyone. Off with their heads!

He said suddenly, inspiration dawning, 'Mary, Queen of Scots. You could do her next. Then flog them together as a pair – her and Elizabeth.'

Neville was smiling at him, looking pleased. 'My dear Craig, what a *brilliant* idea. They never met, of course, but that only makes it all the more *piquant*.'

'She was a silly bitch. Got what was coming to her.'

'I dare say. Some see her rather differently, though. I think we'll give her a tragic look. Perhaps a dear little dog nestling beside her, half-hidden in her skirts. Like the one she took to her execution at Fotheringay Castle. Come over here and we'll do some sketches at once. What sort of colour dress do you think she should have?'

'Royal blue. It'd contrast nice with the red.'

The next hour passed quick as anything while they looked at bits of material and lace and stuff. Then Neville said, 'As a matter of fact, I'm getting rather bored with the country, too. All this snow and mud. Perhaps you're right, dear boy. We ought to think about moving back to London.'

Craig perked up even more. He nodded vigorously in agreement. 'Yes, we ought. But what about your asthma?'

'If anything I think it's worse down here. Dr Harvey recommends a holiday, by the way. Somewhere warm and sunny. What do you think of that?'

'Sounds just the ticket.'

'I thought so too. The Caribbean perhaps, or Mauritius, or maybe the Maldives. It'll do us both good. We'll send for some brochures. Choose somewhere really nice.'

Blimey! He'd never even been out of England, not even on a booze trip to France. Fancy that! A holiday in one of those posh places he'd only ever seen pictures of – blue sea, white sands, waving palm trees, him and Neville dining outside under the stars . . . Come to that, he'd never had a holiday in his life, not of any kind.

They carried on planning Mary, Queen of Scots and her outfit and Craig was chuffed that Neville was treating him like an equal – asking his opinion about everything, listening carefully to what he had to say. After a while, Craig looked at the clock.

'Shall I go and start the supper now?'

'Just as you wish, dear boy. What are we having?'

'There's the fillet steak I've been marinating overnight. We could have a nice green salad with it and I could do some *pommes allumettes*. We've got some fresh fruit for afters. Would that suit you?'

'It all sounds perfectly delicious.' Neville patted his hand. 'Whatever would I do without you?'

'How's your flu coming along, Roger?'

Major Cuthbertson rustled his *Times*. There was no sympathy or concern that he could detect in his wife's enquiry but that was nothing new.

'It seems to be on the mend.'

'That's good because Mrs Hunter just phoned. She wanted to know if you'd help put out the chairs for the talk on The Dorset of Old next week. And put them away afterwards, of course.'

He turned a page. 'What did you say?'

'I told her that of course you would. That's right, isn't it?'

If there was one thing he absolutely hated doing it was heaving chairs around the village hall and being ordered about by a female like Mrs Hunter, who could teach most sergeant majors a thing or two.

The chairs had to be unstacked – wrenched apart from each other like supermarket trolleys – and then set out in perfect rows while Mrs Hunter marched up and down, measuring the space between them with a long stick.

It also meant – even worse – attending a boring talk that would drag on all evening before everyone finally left and the chairs could be carried away and restacked with as much effort as it had been to unstack them.

'Don't think I'm up to it, as a matter of fact.' The major shook his paper again. 'Still a bit wobbly, you know.'

He'd been trawling the Deaths column for people he knew, running a finger down the names. Poor old 'Chalky' White had just dropped off his perch – same age as himself, come to think of it.

His wife said, 'I hear the new people from Brook House are going to be there. The Hanburys. We met them at that drinks before Christmas – you remember?'

By Jove, he remembered all right! Just moved in and the wife was a stunner. She'd given him the eye when they'd been introduced – no doubt about it. Tipped him the wink, if he wasn't much mistaken. The major fingered the knot of his tie. Not quite in the class of Lois Delaney, of course, but still a damned good-looker.

He turned another page and sighed. 'Well, I suppose I'll have to turn out. Do my duty.'

Mrs Cuthbertson gave her guard dog bark of a laugh. As she left the living room, she said over her shoulder, 'Yes, I thought you would, Roger.'

The colonel woke later than usual the next day. When he went downstairs, Thursday had already left his place on the sofa and was waiting for him in the kitchen, sitting accusingly beside his empty *DOG* bowl. The fresh chicken had been finished the day before and so the colonel opened a foil container of ready-prepared cat food. Cod and vegetables in jelly, it said. A delicious and perfectly balanced meal for adult cats. Whatever the manufacturers claimed, Thursday was not impressed. He sniffed at it and walked away towards the back door to be let out.

The colonel went upstairs to shave, shower and dress and came down to fill the kettle and switch it on for coffee. Then he went to fetch the newspaper from the hall mat below. As he walked back to the kitchen, he glanced at the front page.

Tycoon dies in helicopter crash.

Bruce King, the wealthy property tycoon, was killed yesterday when the helicopter he was piloting crashed into a hillside. He had been on his way to attend a business meeting in Glasgow when the weather had unexpectedly deteriorated and he had been blown off-course. Mr King was alone in the machine.

There was an obituary inside. A photograph of Bruce King and a full account of his life from the back-to-back home in a Yorkshire mining town, his early days labouring on building sites, the small bank loan that had enabled him to buy a derelict house, renovate it himself and then sell it in order to buy larger one . . . and so on to the gradual building-up over the years of BHK Group.

His first marriage was mentioned and the death of his only child, a son, at the age of six. The second marriage rated only one line; the third to Lois Delaney several and included the fact that they had recently separated and that a divorce had been in process when she had taken her own life. His wealth was estimated at three hundred million pounds. It was understood that it would be directed to endow a research centre for treatment of cystic fibrosis, to be named in memory of his son, Harry.

The colonel stood drinking his coffee and looking out of the kitchen window. Fate, it seemed, had intervened on Lois Delaney's behalf and administered a rough and summary justice. The biblical eye for an eye, the tooth for a tooth that he had come across before. He had no quarrel with it.

He watched Thursday picking his way gingerly across the sodden lawn. In a moment he would be at the back door, expecting something other than the delicious and perfectly balanced cod and vegetables to be on offer. He must rummage through the store cupboard and find something else to please him.

The hellebores were still waiting patiently in their pots

and today would be a good day to plant them out and give them an encouraging pep talk to start them off. January was a grim month, the colonel thought. Dark, cold, colourless, depressing. Still a long way to go before spring arrived.

He caught sight of some small white dots that had mysteriously appeared under the lilac tree: a delicate fairy ring forming around its base. Damn it, he'd forgotten all about the snowdrops! Between them and the hellebores, things would soon be looking up. He must go and see which of the varieties he'd planted had been the first out of the gate. His money was on *Galanthus nivalis,* the dear old common snowdrop, rather than its classier cousins.

Later on, when he'd finished the planting, he'd walk down to the rough grass at the far end of the garden and check if, by any chance, some of the daffodils were beginning to come through.

And, perhaps in a day or two, when he felt like it, he'd drive over to that reclamation place and find out what they had in the way of old flagstones. Maybe Naomi's sundowner terrace wasn't such a bad idea, after all.